2 DINOSAUR DETECTIVE

Fair Play

To DML. BBC

For my first love, that girl from Paterson. DMD

Text copyright © 1994 by Christina Lowenstein

Illustrations copyright © 1994 by Daniel Mark Duffy

Book design by Debora Smith

Scientific American Books for Young Readers is an imprint of W. H. Freeman and Company, 41 Madison Avenue New York, New York 10010

This book was reviewed for scientific accuracy by Don Lessem, founder of The Dinosaur Society.

Library of Congress Cataloging-in-Publication Data

Calhoun, B. B.

Fair Play / by B. B. Calhoun

—(Dinosaur detective ; #2)

Summary: Fenton Rumplemayer enters the dinosaur science fair and helps solve a mystery at his father's archaeological site.

ISBN 0-7167-6520-9 (hard). —ISBN 0-7167-6531-4 (soft)

[1. Dinosaurs—Fiction. 2. Science Projects—Fiction. 3. Mystery and detective stories. 4. Bullies—Fiction.] I. Title. II. Series: Calhoun, B. B. Dinosaur detective; #2.

PZ7.L9649Fai 1994

[Fic]—dc20

93-37746
CIP
AC

Printed in the United States of America.

10 9 8 7 6 5 4 3 2 1

2 DINOSAUR DETECTIVE
Fair Play

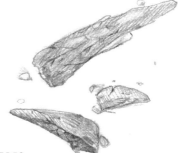

B. B. Calhoun

illustrated by Daniel Mark Duffy

Scientific
BOOKS FOR YOUNG READERS
American

W. H. FREEMAN AND COMPANY ◆ NEW YORK

1

"What do you think it is, Dad?" asked Fenton Rumple-mayer, crouching down to touch a piece of fossilized bone protruding from the huge rock in front of him.

"No way of telling yet, son," answered Bill Rumplemayer. "We'll have to wait and see what shows up after we uncover some more of it."

"It's definitely a dinosaur, though, right?" asked Fenton hopefully. Fenton loved dinosaurs. Back in New York City, the Rumplemayers had lived across the street from the New York Museum of Natural History, where both of Fenton's parents had worked. Fenton had gone there just about every day after school. Now, since his move to Morgan, Wyoming, one of Fenton's favorite things to do was to visit the dig site on Sleeping Bear Mountain, where his father was in charge of a team of paleontologists who were looking for dinosaur fossils.

"Oh, I think we can be pretty sure it's a dinosaur, all right," said Charlie Smalls, another of the paleontologists.

"We'll have to date it to be sure," said Lily Martin, a professor from Wyoming State University who was also working at the dig site, "but I'd guess this is Cretaceous rock."

"So it's somewhere between sixty-five and a hundred and thirty-five million years old," said Fenton. Fenton knew that the Cretaceous was the last period of the Mesozoic Era, the age of dinosaurs. He wondered what kind of dinosaur lay buried beneath the rock. "When can we start uncovering it?"

"Just as soon as we go get the tools," said Charlie, grinning. "Come on, Fenton, why don't you give me a hand?"

Fenton and Charlie walked over to the team's nearby camp and stepped into the trailer that the paleontologists used as an office and supply room. The trailer reminded Fenton of his parents' office at the museum in New York. But it was even more cluttered. Books and papers were crammed onto the rickety metal shelves against one wall, and boxes overflowing with files stood stacked in a corner. The large table in the center of the room held Fenton's father's laptop computer; around it were piles of sketches, snapshots, and pieces of rock.

Fenton noticed a photograph of his mother and picked it up. It showed her sitting in front of a tent, shading her eyes from the sun with her hand. She, like Fenton's father, was a paleontologist. The picture had been taken recently, at a dig site in India, where she was working on a special grant to study dinosaur bones for a year.

Charlie maneuvered his way around the worktable and reached under it.

"Here we are," he said, pulling out two of the red plastic tool kits that held the team's digging equipment. He put the kits down on a chair. "Hey, Fenton, want to try a real taste sensation?"

"Sure," said Fenton, putting down the snapshot.

Charlie leaned over to a nearby shelf and reached into one of the yellow plastic bins where the team kept supplies. He pulled out a purple package and tossed it to Fenton. "Take your pick."

Fenton looked down at the label. "'Bubble Blasters Chewing Gum,'" he read. "'Thirty sticks, fifteen fantastic flavors—watermelon, root beer, blueberry, vanilla, green apple, licorice, coconut, peanut butter, banana, chocolate, popcorn, lemon-lime, marshmallow, mango, caramel.' Wow!"

"Best gum in the world," said Charlie. "I have a friend in California who sends it to me; you can't get it around here. Take your pick."

"Popcorn-flavored bubble gum?" said Fenton incredulously, sliding a piece out of the pack. "This I have to try."

"Great choice," said Charlie, taking the pack back from Fenton. He chose a stick for himself and put the package back in the yellow bin. "I'm kind of partial to the watermelon, myself." He popped a stick of hot-pink gum into his mouth. "Well, let's get this stuff out there and start digging."

Fenton unwrapped his piece of bright yellow gum and bit down on it. Instantly his mouth was filled with the flavor of buttered popcorn.

"This is amazing!" he said, chewing. He reached toward the chair for one of the red tool cases.

"Sure you can handle that, Fenton?" asked Charlie, picking up the other one.

"No problem," said Fenton, straining a little to lift the case.

Fenton and Charlie carried the tool cases back to where Bill Rumplemayer and Lily Martin were waiting and began unpacking the tools. Fenton loved working on uncovering fossils. When he had first gotten to Wyoming, he had helped his father's team uncover some mysterious dinosaur footprints. In fact, it had been Fenton himself who had solved the mystery of the footprints in the end.

Fenton and the others each took a spot on the huge rock and began to work. They started with the larger tools, using picks and scrapers to scoop away the stone that surrounded the imbedded bones, but being careful not to damage any of the bones themselves.

As Fenton dug, he could feel the hot sun beating down on his back. He took his blue bandanna out of his back pocket and wiped his forehead. Uncovering fossils was hard work, but he didn't mind. He was too excited about what lay under the rock to care.

As the afternoon wore on, the piece Fenton was working on began to take shape. It was about a foot and a half long and seemed to be cone shaped. After he had removed the bigger hunks of rock and dirt from the area, Fenton switched to the smaller tools for the more delicate work of separating the remaining bits of stone from the fossil. He scraped at the rock and dirt, using first a small pick and then a dental pick and a paintbrush.

As Fenton exposed the fossil, he saw that it had a fairly sharp point at one end, the narrow end of the cone. The broad end was a little jagged, as if it had been broken off from another piece.

Just then Charlie walked over from his section of the rock to where Fenton was digging.

"Looks like you and I are working on a matched set," said Charlie, peering over Fenton's shoulder.

"Huh?" said Fenton.

"Come take a look," said Charlie.

Fenton followed Charlie over to a section of ground a few yards away. There, still imbedded in the rock, was a fossil almost exactly the same size and shape as the one he had been uncovering.

"What are they?" asked Fenton.

"Well," said Charlie, taking off his big dusty cowboy hat, "they look to me like they could be some kind of horn, or spike."

"Wow," said Fenton. "Then maybe there's a ceratopsid buried here." The ceratopsids were horned dinosaurs. "Aren't these kind of small for ceratopsid horns, though?" he asked. He knew that most ceratopsids would have stood taller than a grown man and grew to at least eighteen feet. Triceratops, one of the largest, was almost thirty feet long. Its horns would have been several times the size of these pieces.

"Probably so," agreed Charlie. "But some ceratopsids had smaller spikes or bony nodules on their frills. Maybe that's what these are."

Fenton nodded. He knew that the enlarged bony sections at the backs of ceratopsids' necks were called frills. Ceratopsid frills had always reminded him of winter coat collars turned up against the wind. The spikes, or nodules, that Charlie was talking about were pointy projections that appeared on the edges of some ceratopsids' frills. Both anchiceratops and styracosaurus were ceratopsids that had them.

"Well, what's going on over here?" asked Fenton's father, brushing his hands off on his pants and walking over to where Fenton and Charlie were standing.

"Looks like Fenton and I have found us a matching pair of pointy-looking bookends," said Charlie, chuckling.

"We think they may be ceratopsid spikes," said Fenton.

"Well, that theory corresponds perfectly with what I've been uncovering over there," called Lily Martin from another part of the rock. "I've found several large pieces of what looks an awful lot like a neck frill of some kind."

"It certainly sounds as if we've got a ceratopsid," agreed Mr. Rumplemayer.

"What kind do you think it is, Dad?" asked Fenton.

"We'll have to wait until we've dug up more of it to know for sure," said Fenton's father. "Let's hope we find enough pieces to be able to identify it."

Fenton looked around, imagining the scene as it might have been millions of years ago. A large, sturdily built ceratopsid of some kind made its way through a clump of plants, foraging for food. It bent down and took a mouthful of leaves, the spikes of its neck frill silhouetted against the sky, and chewed contentedly. But then what had happened? How had the dinosaur died? How had it ended up buried in this particular spot?

"How do you think it died, Dad?" asked Fenton.

"No way of telling, yet, son," said Mr. Rumplemayer.

"But if we're very lucky, the answer is buried somewhere in this rock," said Charlie.

"Well," said Professor Martin, walking over to them, "so far the bones appear to be in something of a jumble. The fact that pieces of the frill and horns were found so far apart from one another might indicate something about the way the animal died."

"Or something about what happened to the animal's body *after* it died," said Mr. Rumplemayer.

"Either way," said Charlie, "it seems like these bones might have a bit of a story to tell us."

Fenton gazed at the mound of rock and thought about all the fossils that could still be hidden inside. He wondered what had happened to the ceratopsid and how it had died. Had it been sick, had some kind of accident, or maybe even been attacked by some other dinosaur? And how had its bones become jumbled together like that? One thing he knew for sure: The only way he could ever hope to get any answers was to keep digging. Until then, exactly what had happened to this dinosaur more than 65 million years ago would definitely remain a mystery.

"Okay," he said, eagerly picking up a small chisel. "I guess it's time to get back to work and see what else we can uncover."

"Feels more like quitting time to me," said Charlie, chuckling.

"I agree," said Professor Martin, taking off her large straw hat. "Let's wrap up for the day."

"Quitting time?" Fenton repeated, astonished. "We can't stop now; we could be on the brink of an amazing discovery!"

"Son, it's five-thirty," said Mr. Rumplemayer, looking at his watch.

"Five-thirty!" said Fenton, amazed. How had the afternoon gone so quickly? Well, he'd just have to wait till tomorrow to do more digging. "Dad, I want to come up here first thing in the morning to work on this some more. I'll ride up with you in the truck when you leave for work, okay?"

"Okay," said his father. "Wait a minute—aren't you forgetting something?"

"What?" asked Fenton.

"Isn't tomorrow Monday, your first day of school?"

"Oh!" said Fenton. Of course, his father was right. Tomorrow he would start sixth grade at Morgan Elementary. He had been so excited about the fossil find that he had completely forgotten. "I guess I'll have to come out after school, then."

Fenton sighed. School had always been okay, but he'd much rather be at the dig site. Besides, he couldn't help feeling a little nervous about the idea of starting a brand-new school. In New York, he'd been in the same class with practically all the same kids since first grade. Here in Morgan, the only person he would know in the whole school would be his neighbor, Willy Whitefox.

Why couldn't Willy be in sixth grade like me? thought Fenton. That would make things so much easier. But Willy was a year younger than Fenton, and would be starting fifth grade tomorrow. Fenton thought about his best friend back in New York, Max Bellman. With Max in his class, Fenton had always known that he would have someone to sit with at lunch, someone to stand with in line.

Fenton gazed longingly at the mound of rock in front of

him. He wished he didn't have to start school tomorrow. In fact, he couldn't help wishing he didn't have to start sixth grade in Morgan at all. It would be so much more fun to spend his days up here at the dig site with the dinosaurs.

2

Later that night Fenton turned on the computer in the second-floor study of the house where he and his father lived, and activated the modem. Keying in Max's number in New York, he thought about how lucky it was that the museum had given his father a computer with a built-in modem to take to Wyoming. Otherwise, he would never be able to play Treasure Quest with Max.

Max was a computer genius, and Treasure Quest was the computer game he had created. Playing it had been one of the boys' favorite things to do back in New York, and now, thanks to the modem, they could continue to play even though they were halfway across the country from each other.

]HI MAX ITS ME[

Fenton typed.

<HI FENTON. HOWS IT GOING?>

came Max's response on the screen.

]PRETTY GOOD. WE FOUND SOME DINO BONES 2-DAY
AT THE DIG SITE. IT LOOKS LIKE A HORNED DINO.
NOW WE R TRYING 2 FIGURE OUT HOW IT DIED[

<**SOUNDS COOL. SCHOOL STARTS 2-MORROW. IM IN
MRS RENNERS CLASS THIS YEAR**>

]TOMORROWS THE 1ST DAY HERE 2. I DONT KNOW MY
TEACHER YET THO[

<**WANT 2 PLAY TQ NOW?**>

]OK[

In five minutes the boys were completely involved in their game. Playing Treasure Quest with Max, Fenton found it was easy to forget his worries about starting school the next day. That is, until he and Max signed off for the night.

]WANT 2 PLAY AGAIN 2-MORROW NITE? IM GOING 2
THE DIG SITE AFTER SCHOOL BUT WE COULD PLAY
LATER[

Fenton keyed in.

<**I MIGHT HAVE A LOT OF HOMEWORK. MAYBE WE
SHOULD WAIT TILL THE WEEKEND**>

Fenton's heart sank. This time tomorrow night, he'd probably be doing homework too. There was no doubt about it; summer was over.

16

]OK. HOW ABOUT SATURDAY?[

he typed reluctantly.

< OK. SAME TIME?>

]RIGHT[

<BYE>

]BYE. HAVE FUN IN MRS RENNERS[

"Fenton! Fenton, are you ready?" Willy called from outside the next morning.

Spooning the last of his cereal into his mouth, Fenton stood up from the table and hurried over to the kitchen window. Willy was in the backyard, straddling his red bicycle.

Fenton gulped down his mouthful of cereal. "Be out in a minute, Willy!" he called through the window.

"Sure you don't want me to give you boys a lift to school in the truck?" asked Fenton's father, rinsing his coffee cup at the kitchen sink.

"Thanks anyway, Dad," said Fenton. "We'll ride our bikes."

Fenton grabbed the paper bag with his lunch in it and raced out of the kitchen, down the hall, up the stairs to the second floor, and into the study, where he clambered up the ladder that hung from the ceiling. He hurried across his attic bedroom, grabbed his stegosaurus backpack off the bed, and stuffed his lunch inside. Jamming his triceratops baseball cap backward onto his head, he started back downstairs.

"Bye, Dad!" he called, banging out the side door and down the porch steps. "Hi, Willy."

"Hi," said Willy. "Come on, Fenton, we'd better get going so we're not late. We don't want to get demerits on our first day."

"Demerits, what are those?" asked Fenton, wheeling his bike out of the garage.

"They're bad marks against you that you get when you do something wrong in school," explained Willy as they took off together down the dirt road. "Kind of like strikes in baseball. Except instead of three, you get four of them before you're out."

"Out?" said Fenton. "What do you mean?"

"Four demerits and you get detention," said Willy.

"Detention, what's that?" asked Fenton.

"It's staying after school," said Willy. "You have to go to the library with all the other kids who are being punished and do schoolwork. You aren't allowed to talk or anything."

"Wow," said Fenton. At his old school in New York there hadn't been anything like that. He certainly hoped he would never have to go to detention.

The boys turned left on the paved road and headed into Morgan and up a side street. In a few minutes Fenton could see

Morgan Elementary ahead. The grass and concrete school yard was filled with kids. Fenton watched them running and yelling or standing in small groups talking.

Fenton and Willy parked their bikes in the bike rack near the school-yard fence right as the bell rang.

"Come on," said Willy. "We're just in time. Sixth grade lines up over there, near the rock." He pointed toward a far corner of the school yard, where a large rock protruded from a patch of grass. Fenton could see a few kids starting to form a line on the pavement nearby.

"See you at lunch!" Willy called, trotting over toward his own line.

As he crossed the school yard by himself, Fenton could hear Willy calling out greetings to some of the other kids. He had never felt so alone. And he was sure that everyone else must be looking at him as he walked toward the line of sixth graders.

He stepped into place in line behind a boy in jeans and a cowboy hat. Nobody in New York ever wore a cowboy hat to school, thought Fenton. Just then the boy turned to him and smiled. Relieved, Fenton smiled back.

Suddenly there was a commotion near the front of the line. He craned his neck to see what was going on.

A tall boy in a white T-shirt was pushing into line in front of a smaller boy.

"Hey, Buster, that's not fair!" squeaked the smaller boy. "I was here."

"That's absolutely right, Franklin," said Buster with a sneer. "You *were* here. But now *I* am. Now, that's not too difficult to understand, is it?"

"Uh, I g-guess not," stammered Franklin, looking down at his sneakers.

"Excellent!" said Buster, smiling wickedly. "Then you won't have too much trouble understanding if I invite a few of my friends to keep me company, either." He cupped his hands and yelled to two boys and a girl who were goofing around near the back of the line. "Hey, you guys, come on over here. I got a spot for us."

Fenton watched in amazement as the three made their way forward.

"Nice going, Buster," said the girl as she stepped into line behind him, along with the smaller of the two boys, who was smiling nervously.

"Yeah, cool," said the taller boy, taking the spot in front of Buster.

"Hey, Matt, what do you think you're doing?" said Buster.

"Huh?" said the taller boy, turning to face him.

"Not *there*," said Buster. "In back of me." He gave Matt a shove. "You *know* you're not supposed to butt in line." He laughed.

"Oh, uh, right," said Matt, forcing a grin.

20

Buster shook his head. "You know, Matt, with a brain like yours, I'm surprised your parents didn't just name you *door*-Matt."

There were a few snickers from kids in the line.

Fenton couldn't believe his eyes. These kids had just cut in front of about fifteen people, and no one was saying anything about it. It seemed like everyone was just going to let them get away with it. Not that Fenton was about to say anything either. The last thing he wanted to do was to start out his first day at a new school by making enemies.

Just then another bell rang, and the lines in the school yard began to snake their way into the red-brick building. Fenton followed the other sixth graders down the hall and into a classroom where a woman with curly dark hair stood behind a desk.

"Good morning, everyone," said the teacher as the students filed in. "Please take a seat."

Fenton looked at the neat rows of desks and chairs. In his old school in New York, the chairs had always been arranged in a circle, so that everyone could see everyone else. Sometimes the kids had even sat on cushions on the floor. He thought about Max starting Mrs. Renner's class in New York without him. The two of them had always sat next to each other; it must be strange for Max, too.

Fenton decided to take a seat in the third row next to the boy with the cowboy hat who had been in front of him in line.

On his other side sat a girl with red hair and freckles, lining up sharpened pencils on the desk in front of her. The boy took off his hat and slipped it under his chair, smiling at Fenton again. As Fenton smiled back, he noticed a red line on the boy's forehead where the hat's band had been.

"Hello, everyone," the teacher began once they were all seated. She looked around the room. "I think I know most of you here, but for those I haven't met, I'm Mrs. Rigby, your homeroom teacher this year. I'll also have you for math and science. Now, the first thing I'd like to do is take the roll and make out a seating chart. Just keep the seats you have for now, and we'll see how it works out."

She opened her roll book.

"I know that some of you have nicknames," she went on, "so, when I say your name, please let me know what you prefer to be called, and I'll mark it down in my book."

As the teacher began calling out the names, Fenton realized that a lot of the kids in the class had nicknames. The boy on his left was Raymond, but was called Ray. The girl on his right, Margaret, was Maggie. And when Mrs. Rigby called Wendell Cregg, Fenton heard a loud, familiar voice from the back snap back harshly.

"That's *Buster!*"

As the teacher made her way down the list toward the *R*'s, Fenton thought about saying that he had a nickname. He had always kind of wanted one. But he couldn't really think of anything. So when Mrs. Rigby called his name, he just answered, "Here."

The morning went pretty quickly. After roll call, Mrs. Rigby wrote out the weekly schedule on the blackboard so the students could copy it into their notebooks. Then she started their math class, which was followed by English with Miss Harding and art with Ms. Schell. When lunchtime came, Mrs. Rigby dismissed the class to the school yard.

"We'll be eating outside as long as the nice weather holds up," she told them.

Eating outside, that sounds fun, thought Fenton. At his old school, they had always eaten in the lunchroom. There hadn't even been a school yard.

Fenton took his paper bag from his knapsack and lined up with the others. The class filed back down the hall and out into the school yard. Several other classes were already out there, and kids had settled around the yard to eat their lunches.

"Hey, Fenton, over here!" came a call.

Fenton saw Willy sitting on a patch of grass near the fence, his lunch bag beside him and a comic book open on his lap.

"How's it going?" asked Willy as Fenton sat down on the grass next to him. "You have Mrs. Rigby, right?"

"Yeah," said Fenton, digging into his paper bag. "She's pretty nice, I guess."

"Mr. Donner's our homeroom teacher," said Willy. "He's strict. He's already given two kids demerits for talking in class."

"Wow," said Fenton, biting into his sandwich.

He looked across the school yard to the grassy area directly opposite. Perched on top of the large rock near the fence, Buster, Matt, and the other two, along with another girl and boy, were eating their lunches.

"Hey, Willy, do you know that guy?" asked Fenton, nodding his head in Buster's direction.

"Buster Cregg? How could I not?" said Willy, rolling his eyes. "If you ask me, he's the nastiest kid in school. But those kids sitting around him are his loyal followers; they think he's really cool." He pointed out the others one by one. "That's Matt Lewis, Jen Wilcox, Jason Nichols, Damian Brown, and Katie Cassidy. They all act like that rock is their personal property."

Fenton watched as Buster tore off tiny bits of paper from his lunch bag and threw them to the ground near where a small bird was standing. Every time the bird pecked at the scraps of paper, thinking they were crumbs of food, Buster and the others would laugh.

"How come he has all those friends if he's so mean?" asked Fenton.

"Well," said Willy, "I don't know much about Matt, Jen, and Jason, but Katie and Damian are in my class. They're pretty much junior jerks themselves. I guess it makes them feel important to hang around with the biggest jerk in the school."

"Buster was definitely a jerk this morning," agreed Fenton.

"He, Matt, Jason, and Jen cut in front of practically the whole line in the school yard."

"Well, I'd definitely steer clear of that gang if I were you," said Willy. "Buster Cregg is definitely not someone you want to have as your enemy. Hey, you want some homemade peanut butter cookies? My mom gave me extra for you."

"Sure, thanks," said Fenton, digging gratefully into the plastic bag that Willy held out. His father had packed him only a sandwich, and his lunch was starting to seem a little skimpy next to Willy's sandwich, apple, carrot sticks, and cookies. He thought about the lunches his mother used to pack him back in New York, the way she sometimes put a note in his bag, telling him to have a good day. He had always been a little embarrassed by the notes, but now, he had to admit, he kind of missed them.

"So," said Willy, "we're going out to the dig site after school, right?"

"Definitely," said Fenton, munching on a peanut butter cookie. "Wait till you see the new fossils. We think they're horns or spikes from a ceratopsid, a horned dinosaur."

"Wow," said Willy. "I can't wait."

"Me neither," said Fenton. "Maybe my father and the others have found enough other bones by now to figure out exactly what kind of ceratopsid it was, and what happened to it."

"What happened to it?" Willy repeated.

"Sure," said Fenton. "Bones can sometimes tell you if a dinosaur was hurt before it died. And the rock you find around the bones can tell you stuff too, like whether there was a volcano."

"Cool," said Willy. "I wish we were at the dig site right now."

"Me too," said Fenton.

Just then the bell rang for the end of lunch, and kids began lining up.

"Okay, see you after school, Willy," said Fenton as they stood up.

"Right," said Willy. "I'll meet you at the bike rack."

The rest of the afternoon went quickly, and finally it was time for the last class of the day, science with Mrs. Rigby.

"The first thing I'd like to talk to all of you about is this year's science fair," said Mrs. Rigby. "As many of you know, the science fair is the first sixth-grade project of the year."

A girl in the front row raised her hand.

"What's the fair going to be about this year, Mrs. Rigby?" she asked.

"Good question, Lisa," said Mrs. Rigby. "I was just getting to that. As most of you know, each year the science fair has a theme. In the past, we've had the Space Exploration Fair and the Inventors' Fair. And then there was last year's Ecology Fair, which was a big success. This year, the sixth grade will be presenting the Dinosaur Fair."

Fenton's eyes widened. A Dinosaur Fair—this was great news!

"We'll talk more about the fair in a couple of days, but now please open your notebooks. I'd like to give you all some background information on dinosaurs," said Mrs. Rigby. She turned to the blackboard. "The dinosaurs lived during the Mesozoic Era, which spanned from two hundred forty-five million years ago to sixty-five million years ago." She drew a time line on the board and labeled the beginning and end of the Mesozoic Era. "The Mesozoic is divided into three periods, the Triassic, the Jurassic, and the Cretaceous."

Fenton quickly copied down the time line in his notebook and happily began sketching a T. rex in the margin. Maybe school would be all right after all.

"Now," Mrs. Rigby went on, "just to put this all into perspective for you, I'm going to fill in the eras before and after the Mesozoic. These are the Paleozoic and the Cenozoic Eras, and they're divided into periods too."

She began to write in the periods of the Cenozoic Era, the time before the dinosaurs, when the first land plants and insects appeared on the earth. Fenton filled in the names of the periods on his own time line: Cambrian, Ordovician, Silurian, Devonian, Carboniferous, Permian. Next Mrs. Rigby wrote in the two periods of the Cenozoic Era, the time after the dinosaurs disappeared: Tertiary and Quaternary.

Suddenly Fenton remembered something, and his hand shot up.

"Yes, uh—Fenton," said Mrs. Rigby, looking down at her seating chart.

"Um, I know a pretty cool way to remember the period names for all three eras," said Fenton.

"Oh really?" said Mrs. Rigby, looking interested.

"Yeah," said Fenton. "'Craterosauruses Often Sit Down Creakily. Perhaps Their Joints Cramp Terribly Quickly,'" he recited.

A few people in the class laughed.

"You see," explained Fenton, grinning, "'Craterosauruses' starts with *C*, which makes you think of Cambrian. 'Often' starts with *O*, for Ordovician. 'Sit' is *S*, for Silurian, 'Down' is *D*, for—"

"For Devonian," said Mrs. Rigby with a smile. "I see, Fenton." She wrote each one of the words from Fenton's sentence next to the corresponding period name on the board. "That's marvelous, Fenton. Did you learn that in your old school?"

"Actually, my friend Charlie taught it to me," said Fenton. "He works with my father up at the dig site at Sleeping Bear Mountain."

"Oh, yes," said Mrs. Rigby. "I heard the university was doing some digging there."

Fenton nodded.

"Well, thank you very much for the memory tool, Fenton," said Mrs. Rigby. "'Craterosauruses Often Sit Down Creakily. Perhaps Their Joints Cramp Terribly Quickly.' I'm sure all of us will remember it now."

"That's for sure," said Buster from the back of the room. "It's so dumb, how could we ever forget it?"

Mrs. Rigby raised her eyebrows. "Well then, Buster, perhaps you have a better memory tool to help us remember the period names?"

"Sure," said Buster, snickering. He paused, squinting at the board. "How about this one? 'Clever . . . Oddballs . . . Show-off During Class. . . . Perhaps They Just . . . Could Try Quitting.'"

A ripple of laughter ran through the class, and Fenton felt his face growing hot. He sank down in his chair, wishing he hadn't said anything.

"That is enough!" Mrs. Rigby said sharply, looking around the room. The laughter died down. "Buster, you've just earned yourself a demerit with that remark."

"What do you mean?" said Buster indignantly. "I didn't do anything wrong! You asked me a question, Mrs. Rigby; all I did was answer it. How can I get a demerit for that?"

"Buster, you know exactly what I'm talking about," said Mrs. Rigby. "That kind of rudeness toward a new student is a poor reflection on all of us." She looked around the room. "I only hope that Fenton won't have the impression that all of the students at Morgan Elementary are this discourteous."

Fenton sank down farther in his seat. *He* only hoped that Mrs. Rigby would stop talking about the whole thing.

"All right," said Mrs. Rigby briskly. "Our time is just about up. We'll talk more about the fair at our next class, on Wednesday. And Buster, before you go, I'd like to talk to you."

The class began gathering their books, and Fenton made his way toward the front of the room.

"Oh, Fenton," said Mrs. Rigby, looking up from her desk, "I'd like to see you, too, for a moment. You can wait out in the hall until I'm finished speaking with Buster."

"Uh, okay," said Fenton, slinging his backpack over his shoulder and going out into the hall. He wondered what it was that Mrs. Rigby wanted to talk to him about. He hoped he wasn't in some kind of trouble. She couldn't blame him for what had happened with Buster, could she?

The rest of the students filed out the door of the classroom and down the hall toward the exit. Fenton looked at his watch. Five after three. He hoped Mrs. Rigby wasn't going to take too long. Willy was probably already waiting for him out by the bike rack. Besides, he was eager to get out to the dig site and see if there was any more news about the ceratopsid and how it had died.

Ten minutes later the door to the classroom opened and Buster came out, a nasty scowl on his face. His frown deepened when he saw Fenton.

"Well, if it isn't Clever Oddball," he hissed under his breath as he went by, "the teacher's pet."

Fenton watched Buster walk down the hall and took a deep breath. He couldn't believe it; somehow he had managed to make an enemy on his first day of school after all. Willy's words to him at lunch echoed through his head: *Buster Cregg is definitely not someone you want to have as your enemy.*

Fenton shuddered. Maybe if he ignored it, this whole thing with Buster would just blow over.

He walked into the classroom and found Mrs. Rigby at her desk.

"Ah, yes, Fenton," she said, looking up with a smile. "Thank you for waiting. I wanted to ask you something."

"Okay, Mrs. Rigby. What is it?" said Fenton.

"I wonder if you think your father might allow the class to take a trip out to the site at Sleeping Bear soon," she said. "It would be a wonderful opportunity, especially now that we're all going to be working on the Dinosaur Fair."

"Sure," said Fenton. "He'd probably say that was okay."

"Wonderful," said Mrs. Rigby. "Maybe you can mention it to him today and let him know that I'll give him a call tonight so we can set it up."

"Okay, Mrs. Rigby. No problem," said Fenton, turning and heading out the door.

Fenton hurried down the hall toward the exit. He glanced

at his watch. Three-twenty—Willy must be wondering where he was.

But when he got outside, Willy was nowhere in sight. Fenton's blue bike stood by itself in the bike rack. Fenton looked around, wondering if Willy had given up and gone home.

As he began to wheel his bike out of the rack, he noticed something; the rear tire was completely flat. He bent down to examine it.

Just then Willy came riding around the corner.

"Hey, Fenton, where were you?" he asked, screeching to a stop and climbing down from his seat. "I waited for a while, but when you didn't show up, I thought maybe you got confused and were waiting near one of the other exits."

"I had to stay late to talk to Mrs. Rigby," said Fenton. "She wants to take the sixth grade on a field trip to Sleeping Bear. Look, I think I have a flat tire."

"Wow," said Willy, leaning his own bike up against the rack. "You sure do." He bent down next to Fenton to look. "Hey, what's this?" He pulled at something small and silver sticking out of the tire. "It looks like a thumbtack."

"A thumbtack?" said Fenton. "How did that get there?"

"Beats me," said Willy. "Maybe you rode over it or something."

Fenton thought a moment.

"Willy, you said you waited for me here for a few minutes, right?" he asked.

"Right," said Willy. "Then, when you didn't show up, I decided to ride around the building."

"Well, when you were here before, was my tire flat?" asked Fenton.

Willy wrinkled his forehead. "I don't think so. At least, I didn't notice it. Why? Do you think someone came out here and stuck that tack in your tire while I was looking for you?"

"I'm beginning to think it's possible," said Fenton. In a way it was farfetched, he knew—after all, no one could be absolutely sure that this was *his* bike. But then again, it was the only bike left in the rack, and he was staying after school to talk to Mrs. Rigby.

"But Fenton, who would want to do that?" asked Willy. "And why?"

Fenton shook his head. That was the problem; right now it was all too easy for him to think of someone who would want to do something like that to him.

3

Two days later, Fenton still hadn't made it out to the dig site. By the time he and Willy had taken his bike to the bike shop on Monday and had the tire repaired, it had been too late to ride out to Sleeping Bear. And the next afternoon it had started to rain, so the paleontologists had been forced to stop work early.

Today, though, Fenton was determined to get to Sleeping Bear. His father had told him that several new bones had been uncovered since Sunday, and that the paleontologists were beginning to think that the dinosaur they had found was a styracosaurus, a type of ceratopsid with an unusual spiked neck frill. The team still had no clue at all to how the dinosaur had died, however, and Fenton was eager to take at look at things for himself.

Finally it was time for science, the last class of the day.

"The first thing I want to do is make an announcement," said Mrs. Rigby. "Tomorrow we will be taking a class trip out to the dinosaur dig site on Sleeping Bear Mountain. Fenton's father has generously agreed to show us around and tell us a little bit about the work they're doing out there."

There were several murmurs of excitement, and Fenton couldn't help feeling a little proud. It would be fun to have the class visit the dig site.

For the next half hour Mrs. Rigby talked to them some more about dinosaurs, explaining that there were two main groups of dinosaurs, the saurischians and the ornithischians, and that the best way to tell an ornithischian skeleton from a saurischian skeleton was by the different structures of their hip bones. Ornithischians had hips like birds'; saurischians had hips like lizards'. In addition, the ornithischians were all herbivores—plant eaters—while the saurischians included both meat eaters and plant eaters. Finally, each of the ornithischians had a beaklike bone in front of its teeth.

Fenton started to draw a beaklike bone in his notebook. Almost immediately the sketch turned into a styracosaurus, which, like other ceratopsids, was a member of the ornithischian group of dinosaurs. Suddenly Fenton couldn't wait for class to be over so he could get out to the dig site and see the new styracosaurus bones. He looked at his watch. Two-fifty—ten more minutes.

"Okay, class," said Mrs. Rigby. "Now that you have some basic information to work from, I'd like to talk to you about the Dinosaur Fair. You'll be working on your projects in pairs, and prizes will be awarded to the best projects. Of course, exactly what aspect of dinosaurs you decide to concentrate on is up to you, but the more well thought out and well researched your project is, the better chance you and your partner will have of winning a prize."

Right away Fenton was determined to have one of the prize-winning projects. The only question was who to ask to be his partner. He looked around the room. Picking a good partner was essential. Back in New York, he and Max had made an agreement to be partners for everything. Maybe he should ask Ray, the guy with the cowboy hat. He seemed like he might be pretty nice. Or there was Peter, the boy in the second row who seemed to know the answer to practically every question during math. He would probably be a good partner for a science project.

"Now," said Mrs. Rigby, "before I dismiss you, I'd like to pair up the partners for the projects." She picked up a pad and a pen.

What does she mean? thought Fenton. Don't we get to pick our own partners? In his old school, the kids had always done the choosing.

But as Mrs. Rigby began to pair up teams, Fenton realized that she was matching people with the kids sitting next to them. So it looked like he'd probably get Ray as his partner after all. But he'd guessed wrong.

"Maggie Carr and Fenton Rumplemayer," said the teacher, making a note on her pad.

Fenton looked at the red-haired girl to his right, who glanced briefly at him and smiled before turning her attention back to the teacher. He had to admit, he was a little disappointed. He had never been partners with a girl for anything. Somehow he just didn't think he got along as well with them as with boys. Besides, weren't boys usually more interested in dinosaurs? What if she didn't care as much as Fenton did about the Dinosaur Fair?

Well, he thought, I can probably come up with a good project no matter who my partner is. After all, I've been studying dinosaurs for practically my whole life. I'll just have to think of a really great idea.

"All right," said Mrs. Rigby after she had finished assigning partners. "That's it for today. Now I expect each set of partners to get started on their project idea as soon as possible. After all, the fair is in less than two weeks. See you all tomorrow."

Finally, thought Fenton, time to ride out to Sleeping Bear. As he hurriedly stuffed his books into his backpack, Maggie turned to him.

"So, I guess we should meet to talk about what we want to do for our project," she said.

Fenton looked up.

"Uh, yeah, sure," he said. "Maybe tomorrow or something, okay?"

Maggie raised her eyebrows once quickly and shrugged.

"Fine," she said, turning her back abruptly and beginning to pack her own books.

Great, thought Fenton. Now this girl's mad at me too. It was starting to seem like all he was doing in his new school was making enemies. Well, she would just have to understand. At this point he wasn't about to let anything get in the way of going out to the dig site. Besides, he needed a day or so to come up with a good project idea anyway.

A little over half an hour later, Fenton and Willy were at the dig site, looking at the new bones.

"As you can see, we've found several more spikes, as well as a few more pieces of the skull and a couple of bone fragments from one of the back legs," explained Fenton's father, indicating an arrangement of fossils on the ground beside the excavation site.

Fenton looked at the fossils, which included the two spikes that he and Charlie had found, as well as several more of varying sizes. He could see why the team had identified the dinosaur as a styracosaurus. Styracosauruses had bone nodules that went all the way around the edges of their neck frills, becoming longer as they worked their way around to the back and eventually turning into extended spikes behind their skulls.

"But you still don't have any idea how it died, right?" asked Fenton.

"That's right," said his father. "So far our biggest clue is the fact that this rock it's buried in is sandstone, which means that it may once have been at the sandy bottom of a river."

"A river? Does that mean the dinosaur drowned?" asked Willy.

"Could be," said Charlie, who was digging at a portion of the rock nearby. "But we can't be sure. The dinosaur could have ended up in the river *after* it died."

"And we may never know," said Fenton's father.

"We can still hope for a good clue, though," said Charlie. "There's still lots of this rock to dig up."

"If we're lucky, it could end up being a fairly complete fossil find," said Lily Martin, who was also digging.

"Which would be great news for the museum back in New York," added Fenton's father, "since they don't have a styracosaurus in their collection."

"Oh, that's right," said Fenton, remembering. The only styracosaurus in the museum was a model one third the size of an actual styracosaurus; he had made several sketches from it. Suddenly he was really excited at the possibility of being able to see a complete skeleton. "So, can Willy and I help you dig?"

"Sure," called Charlie from where he was working. "Grab some tools and get busy."

"Cool!" said Willy.

For the next hour or so Fenton and Willy dug away at sections of the rock, first with the larger tools, and then with the smaller picks and brushes. Time flew by as Fenton began to uncover what was starting to seem like an interestingly shaped fossil piece. It had a pointy section at one end, so his first guess was that it would turn out to be yet another spike from the frill, but as he dug farther, he saw that the fossil had a curved shape to it, rather than the straight, conelike shape of the spikes. The more he uncovered, the more curious he became.

"Well," said Charlie, standing up and brushing the dirt off his pants, "what do you say we call it a day?"

"Good idea," said Fenton's father.

"Aw, Dad," said Fenton, "can't I just work on this piece a little longer?"

"Really," said Willy. "I've hardly uncovered anything of mine."

"Sorry, son, but we've got to get going. I need to stop by the auto-repair shop and pick up a part for the truck before they close," said Fenton's father.

"How about if I meet you at home, instead?" said Fenton. "I just want to do a little more on this piece. Willy and I can ride down the mountain on our bikes."

"Well, all right," said Mr. Rumplemayer. "But don't stay too long. I want you home before it starts to get dark. And make sure you put your tools back in the trailer before you leave."

"No problem, Dad," said Fenton.

"Thanks, Mr. Rumplemayer," said Willy.

Ten minutes later the paleontologists were gone. Fenton and Willy stood at the excavation site by themselves.

"Willy, how'd you like to help me out?" asked Fenton.

"You mean with the fossil you're working on? Sure," said Willy. "I haven't really uncovered much over here anyway."

"Well, I've definitely found something pretty interesting," said Fenton. He squatted down by the partially exposed fossil and showed it to Willy.

"Wow," said Willy. "What do you think it is?"

"I don't know," said Fenton. "But there's only one way to find out." He picked up the small pick he had been using. "Come on."

Fenton and Willy set to work, and as the fossil became more exposed, Fenton was intrigued by what he saw. It was curved, and its surface was very smooth, except for a small, hard chunk of something that was stuck to the pointy end.

As they chipped away at it and Fenton began to recognize its shape, he couldn't believe his eyes. Finally the fossil was completely exposed. Now there was no doubt.

"Oh my gosh," said Fenton under his breath. He lifted the curved fossil carefully in his hand.

"What is it?" asked Willy.

"I think it's a claw," said Fenton slowly.

"A claw?" asked Willy. "You mean from the dinosaur?"

"Well, from *a* dinosaur," said Fenton. "But not from the dinosaur we've been uncovering. Styracosauruses didn't have claws like this." He looked at the fossil again. "No, this claw is definitely from a predator."

"A predator?" said Willy. "You mean a meat eater?"

"Exactly," said Fenton. "In fact, I'm pretty positive it's from a member of the dromaeosaurid family, something like a velociraptor or deinonychus."

Fenton examined the claw. He knew that one of the special characteristics of dromaeosaurids, one of the things that made them recognizable, was the fact that they had large, curved claws on the second toes of their back feet. It was thought that they used these claws as hunting weapons.

But what was that small hard chunk on the end? Maybe it was a piece of rock. Fenton scraped at it a little with a dental pick, but it didn't budge; it seemed pretty strongly wedged onto the point of the claw.

"So, does this mean there's *another* kind of dinosaur buried here?" asked Willy.

"It looks that way," said Fenton. "But what I don't understand is how these two different dinosaurs ended up getting buried in the same place. I mean, I guess the dromaeosaurid could have attacked the styracosaurus, but then what killed the dromaeosaurid? It just doesn't make sense."

"Well, however it happened, I bet your father and the others are going to be really excited when they find out that you discovered part of another dinosaur," said Willy.

"Yeah," said Fenton, grinning.

"Hey," said Willy, looking up at the sky, "we'd better get going. We're supposed to be back down the mountain before dark."

"Okay," said Fenton. "I'll be ready in a sec. Let me just put these tools away."

He picked up the tools he and Willy had been using and headed toward the trailer, the claw still in his hand. Maybe he should ride back home with it and show it to his father right away, he thought. But no, it was probably better to leave it somewhere at the dig site, somewhere where all the paleontologists would see it in the morning.

Fenton went into the trailer and looked around. He could leave the claw on the worktable. Someone was bound to notice it there the next day. But then he had an idea; it would be a lot more fun if he could show everyone his discovery himself. Maybe he would just stash it somewhere for now. Then he could ride back out after school the next day and unveil his discovery.

Fenton took his blue bandanna out of his back pocket, wrapped it carefully around the fossil, and looked around. The only question was where to hide it.

His eye was caught by the row of bright yellow storage boxes on the shelf. Perfect—he'd just stick it in one of the yellow bins for now and retrieve it when he came back the next day.

He couldn't wait to see the looks on the team's faces when they realized what he had found.

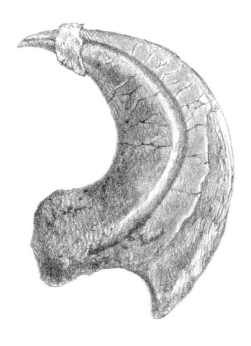

4

The next day, Mrs. Rigby's sixth-grade class stood in front of the mound of rock and partially excavated bones at the Sleeping Bear Mountain dig site. Charlie was on his knees nearby, digging with a small pick, while Mr. Rumplemayer explained the work they were doing to the class.

"All this rock we've been digging up is sandstone," said Fenton's father, "which leads us to believe that this area may once have been the bottom of a river."

"Then where's the river now?" asked Lisa, the girl who usually sat in the front of the classroom.

"It's not here anymore," explained Mr. Rumplemayer. "This area has changed a great deal in the millions of years since these dinosaurs died."

"Yeah," said Fenton. "Sleeping Bear Mountain wasn't even around back then."

"A river may once have flowed through the exact spot you're all standing on," said Charlie, looking up from his work.

"Help! Help! I'm drowning!" cracked Buster. A few students chuckled.

"Buster, that's enough," said Mrs. Rigby. "Mr. Rumplemayer, if there was a river here, do you have any idea of how the dinosaur bones you've been finding might have ended up in it?"

"Well, it's not uncommon for an animal to die on a riverbank and be swept into the water when the river rises," said Fenton's father. "But so far, in this case, it's impossible for us to tell whether the dinosaur got into the river before or after it died."

"So it may have even been the water that killed it," said Franklin.

"Maybe," said Fenton's father.

However it died, it wasn't alone, thought Fenton with a smile. He pictured the dromaeosaurid claw, tucked away in the yellow box in the trailer. He couldn't wait until the afternoon, when he would show his father and the team this latest clue.

"What kind of dinosaur is it?" asked Peter.

"Well, the bones we have found so far seem to indicate that it's a styracosaurus," said Fenton's father.

"A styra-*what?*" asked Ray.

"Styracosaurus," said Mr. Rumplemayer again, more slowly.

"It's one of the ceratopsid family of dinosaurs," added Fenton.

"Those are the horned dinosaurs, right?" said a girl's voice. "Like triceratops?"

Fenton turned to look. It was Maggie Carr.

"Yeah," said Fenton, kind of impressed that she had known that.

"Hey, look at me!" said Buster, picking up a dental pick that was lying on the ground near where Charlie was working. He held the pick up to his forehead. "I'm a triceratops, watch out!" He pawed the ground with one foot like a bull and charged toward Jason, who yelped and jumped out of his way. Matt and Jen burst into laughter.

"Um, actually—" Fenton began.

"Buster Cregg, put that tool back where you found it right now before someone gets hurt," said Mrs. Rigby angrily. "You've just earned another demerit, young man. Now, I'd watch my behavior from now on if I were you. That is, if you don't want to spend an afternoon in detention."

Buster dropped the tool onto the rock surface with a clatter.

What a jerk, thought Fenton.

Mr. Rumplemayer cleared his throat.

"Uh, maybe this is a good time to walk over to the trailer and take a look at what Professor Martin's been working on," he said.

"Sounds like a good idea," said Charlie, standing up. "I'll head over there with you, give these legs a little stretch." He took off his hat and wiped his forehead. "I think we have some sodas over there too. Anybody besides me feel like a cool drink?"

He was answered by an enthusiastic chorus of yeses from the class. The group made its way over to the trailer, Mrs. Rigby asking Mr. Rumplemayer more about the fossil find. When they got there, Charlie went inside and came out with a big blue plastic cooler.

The trailer wasn't large enough to hold everyone at once, so Mrs. Rigby split the class into three groups. Fenton and his father went in with the first group, while Charlie handed out cold sodas to the kids who were waiting outside.

Lily Martin was sitting at the table in the center of the trailer, making sketches. Laid out on the table in front of her were several pieces of bone. Fenton recognized the spikes and pieces of skull he had seen by the excavation site the day before.

"Hello, everyone," said Professor Martin, looking up from her work as the group filed in around the table.

"Professor Martin is measuring and sketching these fossil pieces from the skull to make a record of them," Mr. Rumplemayer explained.

"There are still some pieces missing," said Professor Martin. She picked up two sections of bone and fitted them together. The two pieces lined up perfectly except for a small triangular gap in one area. "For example, we haven't been able to find this piece here, which would have been in the area somewhere below the dinosaur's left eye. When the skull is fully reconstructed, the styracosaurus skull should look like

50

this." She reached for a sketch on the table.

"What are those spiky things for?" asked Peter.

"Were they like weapons?" someone else wanted to know.

"Actually, these spikes on the frill were more likely used as some sort of visual display," said Professor Martin. "To scare off rival styracosauruses or to attract mates."

"You mean they didn't use them to attack and kill other dinosaurs?" asked Ray.

"Probably not," said Fenton.

"Ceratopsids were all herbivores, vegetarians," added Maggie. "So they had no reason to fight unless they were attacked."

Fenton turned to look at her, surprised again by what she had said. He had to admit, he was kind of impressed. He gazed at her curiously, but Maggie kept her eyes on the drawing on the table.

"Well," said Fenton's father, "I guess we'd better go outside and give the next group a chance to take a look. Thank you, Professor Martin."

They filed outside, where Charlie gave them all cold sodas from the cooler. They waited while first Mrs. Rigby and then Charlie went in with the two remaining groups. The sun was hot, and a few of the kids went to wait on the other side of the trailer, where there was some shade.

Fenton leaned up against the trailer in the shade, drinking his soda. He looked at Maggie, who was sitting on a rock nearby, chugging her own soda, and wondered how she knew so

51

much about ceratopsids. Maybe he should go talk to her now, he thought. After all, they were supposed to be planning what to do for the Dinosaur Fair, right? Before, it had seemed pretty obvious that Fenton ought to be in charge of the project. But now Fenton wasn't so sure.

Just then Buster came around the corner of the trailer, chewing gum and tossing a rock in the air as he walked. Matt Lewis loped along a few feet behind him. Suddenly Buster turned to Matt and chucked him the rock.

"Think fast, Matt!" he said, the usual evil grin spreading across his face.

But it was too late. Before Matt even realized what was happening, the rock had grazed his shoulder and hit the ground.

"Ow," he said, rubbing the spot the rock had hit. "Buster, that kind of hurt."

Buster laughed, shaking his head.

"Matt," he said, "take my advice and don't ever go out for baseball. You have the reflexes of a—" He looked around and cracked a smile. "—of a big, dumb brontosaurus."

Matt hung his head and didn't say anything.

What a jerk, thought Fenton again. He could insult his supposed friend *and* an extinct animal all in the same breath.

Fenton crumpled his empty soda can in disgust. He was getting pretty sick of Buster's annoying comments. Someone should really tell Buster off, he thought. Someone should just step right up to Buster and—

Suddenly he saw Maggie stand up from her rock.

"Apatosaurus," she said, turning to face Buster.

"Excuse me?" said Buster, raising his eyebrows. "Are you talking to me, Maggie Carr?"

"Yes I am," said Maggie, putting her hands on her hips. "I said 'apatosaurus.'"

Buster stared at her.

"The correct term for the dinosaur you are thinking of is apatosaurus, not brontosaurus," Maggie went on. "And for your information, apatosaurus and the other sauropods were great successes. So they can't have been too stupid. If you ask me, Buster, I'd say that what was really dumb was throwing a rock at someone like that."

Fenton was amazed. Not only did Maggie know about ceratopsids, and now sauropods, but she was the only person Fenton had seen stand up to Buster.

Buster seemed less impressed.

"Well, no one's asking you, *Gaggie*," he sneered, taking a step toward her. "So why don't you just butt out?"

Fenton looked around, wondering what he should do.

Fortunately, at that moment Mrs. Rigby walked into view. Seeing her, Buster backed off, giving Maggie one last nasty glance.

"It's time to go now," said Mrs. Rigby. "You can all line up and start back to the bus. I'll be there in a minute; I just want to thank Mr. Rumplemayer and the others."

Fenton walked around the trailer, still amazed by what he had seen. Maggie had stood up to Buster without so much as a flinch. Fenton waved good-bye to his father and the others as the class lined up, and slipped into place behind Maggie. As the line made its way toward the school bus, he tried to think of something to say to her.

Fenton climbed on board the bus behind Maggie and realized that there was some sort of argument going on in the third row.

Peter stood in the aisle pleading with Buster, who was sitting with his arms folded across his chest.

"Can't you *please* just move your backpack?" begged Peter, indicating the bright yellow school bag with the big purple stain taking up the window seat next to Buster.

"No, I can't," said Buster. "So I guess you'll just have to find another seat, won't you? There's plenty of room in the back."

"Please, Buster," said Peter again. He lowered his voice. "I get sick if I ride in the back of the bus."

"That's disgusting!" roared Buster. "If you get carsick, you're definitely not sitting next to me, Peter. Or should I just call you *Puker?*"

A few of the kids sitting nearby giggled nervously, and Fenton watched as Peter's face turned red.

"Here," said Lisa, who was sitting across the aisle from Buster. "You can have my seat, Peter. I'll sit in the back."

"Thanks," said Peter, looking relieved.

"Just make sure you keep your face pointed away from me, Puker," said Buster.

"What a complete jerk," said Fenton under his breath as he made his way behind Maggie down the aisle.

Maggie turned to look at him briefly over her shoulder.

"Total creep," she agreed, making her way into a window seat near the back.

Fenton slid into the seat beside her.

"What drives me nuts is that he gets away with it," Maggie went on. "He thinks he's so tough and cool, but he's just plain nasty. Everybody's scared to stand up to him."

"You didn't seem too scared back there near the trailer," said Fenton.

Maggie shrugged.

"I was angry," she said. "When I get mad I can't always stop myself from saying what I think."

Mrs. Rigby climbed on board and the bus started with a lurch.

"Hey," said Fenton, "by the way, how did you know all that stuff about dinosaurs?"

"What stuff?" asked Maggie.

"You know," said Fenton. "About the ceratopsids, and apatasaurus."

"Oh, that," said Maggie. "I read a lot."

"About dinosaurs?"

"About everything," she told him. "I love to read."

"Listen," said Fenton. "Maybe we should get together soon and talk about what we want to do for our project for the Dinosaur Fair."

Maggie looked at him.

"Well, all right," she said. "How about after school?"

Fenton thought for a moment. He had planned on riding back out to the dig site after school to show his father the claw, but he didn't want to put Maggie off again. Besides, he was beginning to get really excited about working with her on the project. Well, maybe there would be time to go to the dig site after he met with Maggie.

"Okay," said Fenton.

Just then they heard Mrs. Rigby raise her voice in the front of the bus. "Buster Cregg, you've just earned yourself a demerit. Take that chewing gum out of your mouth this instant!"

"What do you mean, Mrs. Rigby?" said Buster indignantly. "We're not in school now!"

"School rules apply to field trips as well," said Mrs. Rigby. "No gum chewing allowed."

"That's not fair," whined Buster.

"Buster, one more demerit and you'll be in detention," said the teacher.

"Okay, okay," Buster grumbled, standing up to throw his gum out the window.

Maggie looked at Fenton.

"Complete jerk," she said, nodding her head toward the front of the bus.

"Total creep," he agreed, grinning at her as the bus made its way down the mountain.

5

After school that day Fenton and Maggie headed toward the bike rack at the edge of the school yard, where Willy was waiting.

"Hi," said Fenton, reaching for his bike. "Willy, this is—"

"Hi, Willy, how're you doing?" asked Maggie, wheeling her bike out of the rack.

"Hi, Maggie," said Willy.

"You guys know each other already?" asked Fenton in surprise.

Willy laughed. "Sure. Most of the kids from Morgan know each other at least a little bit, Fenton. Besides, Maggie lives out kind of near us."

"Oh," said Fenton. "Maggie and I are going to have a meeting to talk about our project for the Dinosaur Fair."

"Cool," said Willy, throwing one leg over his bike. "I wish the fifth grade had a science fair. Hey, maybe I can help you guys out with your project."

"Great," said Maggie, climbing up on her bike.

"Let's go to my house," said Fenton as they rode out of the school yard. "I've got a lot of books on dinosaurs that we can use if we need them."

"Fenton's got a huge dinosaur library," agreed Willy.

"Okay, sounds good," said Maggie. "But I have to stop home first and take care of my horse."

Fenton's eyes widened. "You have a horse?"

"Sure," said Maggie, laughing. "My family raises horses."

Suddenly Fenton remembered—the big horse ranch down the road from the turnoff to where he and Willy lived. Willy had told him it was called the Carr Ranch. Wasn't Maggie's last name Carr?

"You guys can come too, if you want," said Maggie.

"Okay," said Fenton. He had never been to a horse ranch. Then he remembered something his father had said to him that morning. "But I have to stop at the Morgan Market and pick up a couple of things."

"The market? Why?" asked Maggie. "What kind of things?"

"Oh, just some stuff for dinner," said Fenton. He reached into his T-shirt pocket. "My dad gave me the list this morning."

"*You* do the food shopping?" asked Maggie, raising her eyebrows in disbelief.

Fenton felt his cheeks flush. "Well, yeah, sometimes. I mean, my mom's out of the country working for a while, so it's just me and my father at home right now. We try to help each other out with cooking and shopping and junk." Suddenly he felt embarrassed. Maybe Maggie would think he was weird because he went grocery shopping.

"That's wild," said Maggie. "My sister and I are practically not even allowed in our kitchen. Even if I just walk in and open the refrigerator, our cook, Dina, asks me what I want."

"You have a cook?" asked Fenton.

"Yeah," said Maggie. "The ranch is really big, so we have a lot of people who work for us. Sometimes it seems like there's somebody there to do *everything* for me. That's what I love about Pepper, my horse; he's the one thing I'm totally responsible for."

Fenton thought about this. In one way, having people around to help you with stuff must be great. It sure would make things easier if he and his father had a cook. On the other hand, he always felt kind of proud when he and his father managed to cook dinner together.

"I guess Willy and I can go to the Morgan Market while you stop home," he said to Maggie. "Then we can meet at my house afterward."

"Fenton's is the white house next to mine," explained Willy.

"Okay," called Maggie, pushing off on her bike. "I'll see you there in about forty-five minutes."

Fenton and Willy hopped on their bikes and took off the other way, toward the Morgan Market.

A few moments later, as they approached the dirt parking lot in front of the Wadsworth Museum of Rocks and Other Natural Curios, Willy rode up next to Fenton.

"Look," he said. "There's Mrs. Wadsworth."

Fenton turned and saw the old woman who ran the museum, dressed as usual in a pair of faded blue overalls. Her white hair was in a knot on the top of her head, and she wore her half-moon spectacles. She was crouching down on the front step of the small red building, peering into the bushes around the steps.

"Come on," said Fenton. "Let's ride over and say hello."

Fenton liked visiting Mrs. Wadsworth. Her museum wasn't like anything he had ever seen in New York. It was tiny, really more like a house than a museum. But it was crammed full of interesting things that Mrs. Wadsworth had collected—teeth, bones, and skulls from animals, as well as feathers, birds' nests, and of course rocks.

"Hi, Mrs. Wadsworth," said Willy as the boys pulled up beside her.

"Well, hello, Willy. Hello, Fenton," said Mrs. Wadsworth, looking up at them and smiling.

"What are you doing?" asked Fenton. "Did you lose something?"

"Yes, actually, I did," said Mrs. Wadsworth. "And I can't understand it."

"What is it?" asked Willy.

"An iguana skull," said Mrs. Wadsworth. "I got it from Mr. Peters over at the pet shop. One of his iguanas died, and he was nice enough to save it for me. I set it out here in the sun to bleach yesterday, but this morning it was gone. I keep coming out to look for it again, hoping it will turn up somehow."

"Maybe we can help you for a minute," said Willy.

"Oh, that's all right, boys," said Mrs. Wadsworth, sighing and standing up. "I've already given the area a thorough search. I thought I'd come out to look one more time, just in case. But I suppose it's gone. Why don't you come in and have a cool drink, though?"

"Thanks, Mrs. Wadsworth, but I don't think we have time," said Fenton. "We have to go to the market and then get home."

"Yeah," said Willy. "We're working on a project for the sixth-grade science fair; this year it's the Dinosaur Fair."

"The Dinosaur Fair, that sounds marvelous!" said Mrs. Wadsworth. She opened the front door to the museum. "Well, good luck with your project, boys."

"Thanks, Mrs. Wadsworth. Bye," said Fenton as she stepped inside. He turned to Willy. "Come on. We'd better pick up the groceries and get to my place."

"Hold on a second," said Willy, putting his hand on Fenton's arm. "Look who's coming."

Fenton turned and looked down the street. Heading toward them were Buster and Matt.

"What are they doing here?" asked Fenton.

"Well, they both live nearby, and they hang out at the lumberyard. Buster's uncle owns it," said Willy, pointing to a building two doors down from Mrs. Wadsworth's. "There's this old abandoned storage building in the back that they use as a clubhouse."

"Let's get going before they see us," said Fenton. "That guy definitely seems to have something against me."

Quickly Fenton and Willy got back on their bikes and rode out of the parking lot. A few minutes later they had finished the shopping, stuffed the groceries into their backpacks, and were on their way home.

They rode up the paved road out of Morgan and turned off at the dirt road that led toward their houses. Fenton led the way up his driveway, and the two boys leaned their bikes against the house and headed inside.

"Phew!" sighed Fenton, dropping his backpack on the kitchen table and opening the yellow refrigerator door. "I'm thirsty."

"Me too," said Willy, pulling out a chair. "What do you have to drink?"

"Not much," said Fenton, picking up an almost empty orange-juice container from the top shelf and shaking it. "I guess we forgot to put juice on the list this morning."

"We could make lemonade," said Willy, pointing at a bag of lemons on the bottom shelf of the refrigerator.

"Cool," said Fenton, reaching for the bag. He had never actually made lemonade before. He was hot and thirsty, though, and cold lemonade sounded delicious.

Fenton put the groceries away, and the two boys began cutting the lemons.

Then Fenton heard Maggie's voice at the side door. "Hello?"

"In here!" he called out.

Maggie walked into the kitchen and flopped down on one of the yellow chairs by the table. "Hi," she said. "What are you doing?"

"Hi," said Fenton. "Making lemonade."

"Want to help?" asked Willy.

"Sure," she answered, standing up and walking over to them at the counter. "What do I do? I've never made lemonade."

"Actually, neither have I," said Fenton, grinning. "I guess Willy's in charge."

Willy rolled his eyes. "I can't believe you guys," he said. "I thought *everyone* knew how to make lemonade."

Maggie and Fenton looked at each other and shrugged.

"Okay," said Willy. "Maggie, you finish squeezing these lemons. Fenton, you go find the sugar."

A few minutes later, they were sitting at the kitchen table, drinking tall glasses of ice-cold lemonade.

"Your father's dig is really cool," said Maggie. "I wish we

could do a project that really shows people what it's like to dig for dinosaurs."

"But how could you do that?" asked Willy. "The fair's in the school gym. You can't exactly bring everyone out to the dig site."

"No," said Fenton, "but maybe we can think of a way to bring the dig site to the fair."

"I know," said Maggie. "We could make a model. We can think of some way to bury bones in it and let people work on digging them out for themselves."

"I'm sure my father would let us borrow some of the tools from the dig site," said Fenton.

"But where are you going to get the dinosaur bones?" asked Willy.

"I don't know," said Fenton, thinking. "I guess maybe we'll have to use some other kind of bones."

"Hey," said Maggie, "how about chicken bones?"

"Chicken bones?" repeated Willy.

"Yeah, I guess that would work," said Fenton. "After all, birds are descended from meat-eating dinosaurs."

"We have chicken at the ranch once a week," said Maggie. "I could ask Dina to save the bones for us."

"Perfect," said Fenton. "Now the only question is what to bury them in. It should be something pretty hard, something that's like rock, so that people can really chip away at it with the tools."

"How about plaster?" suggested Willy.

"Plaster?" said Fenton.

"Sure," said Willy. "Plaster of paris. It's this white powder that you mix with water and it turns really gooey. But when it dries it's hard. Our class was using it yesterday in art with Ms. Schell. We made plaster casts of our hands."

"Like a cast for a broken leg?" asked Fenton.

"Sort of," said Willy. "You take these pieces of gauze and dip them into the plaster, and then you put them all over your hand. When it hardens, you can take it off, and it's the exact shape of your hand."

"It sounds great," said Fenton. "We could just pour the liquid plaster around the chicken bones and let it harden. Maybe we can ask Ms. Schell if she'll let us use some."

"You should probably do the asking, Fen," said Maggie. "I'm really bad in art, and I don't think Ms. Schell likes me much."

"Fenton's a really great artist," said Willy. "He draws amazing dinosaurs. You should see his sketchbooks."

"Can I?" asked Maggie.

"Sure," said Fenton. "I'll go upstairs and get them."

Fenton was secretly pleased that Willy had mentioned his sketchbooks. Back in New York, Fenton had gone to the museum practically every day to draw the dinosaurs. He had filled six sketchbooks with his drawings, and he was kind of proud of them.

"Wow," said Maggie as she leafed through the first of the sketchbooks, "these are great. Nice apatasaurus. Did they really do that, though?"

"Maybe not," admitted Fenton, looking over at the drawing Maggie was examining. It showed an apatosaurus rearing up on its hind legs, balancing to nibble a leaf from a high branch. "The museum put the skeleton in that pose, but a lot of scientists disagree with it. They say that an apatosaurus might not really have been able to balance in that position."

"Still, it's a cool drawing," said Maggie. "It makes me want to show it to all those people who say that dinosaurs were dumb and clumsy—like Buster Cregg."

"Yeah," said Fenton. "Buster thinks he's so cool, but he definitely doesn't know what he's talking about when it comes to dinosaurs."

"You should have seen him, Willy," said Maggie. "He was acting like such a jerk today. He even threw a rock at Matt Lewis."

"Matt's crazy to be friends with him," said Willy.

"What about when he said he was a triceratops and tried to gore Jason Nichols with that digging tool?" said Fenton. "He seems to treat all his friends really badly."

"Yeah, and he's mean to people who aren't his friends too," said Maggie. "Like when he called me Gaggie, or like that first day in science when he made fun of that cool memory tool you told us about, Fen."

67

"Yeah," said Fenton. "And the way he embarrassed Peter on the bus today."

"Oh, that was awful," said Maggie. She turned to Willy. "Poor Peter gets carsick if he rides in the back of the bus, and Buster wouldn't move his backpack to give Peter a seat up front. It made me want to just kick that dirty yellow backpack of his right off the seat."

Suddenly her face changed.

"That's funny. . . ." she said.

"I don't think so," said Willy. "I bet I would have felt the same way."

"No, not that," said Maggie. "It's just that I got off the bus behind Buster when we arrived at the dig site, and I didn't see him carrying a backpack."

"He must have had it," said Fenton. "Otherwise, where did it come from?"

"Probably he got Matt or Jason or Jen to carry it for him at first," said Willy. "Those kids are like Buster's robots or something; they'll do anything he tells them to."

"Yeah," said Maggie, "I guess you're right. Anyway, Fen, these drawings are great." She turned a page. "Hey, this one's a styracosaurus, right? Like out at the dig site."

"Right," said Fenton. "I did it from a model of one back at the museum in New York. They don't actually have a styracosaurus skeleton in their collection. At least, not yet. After my father and the others finish digging this one up they will, though."

"Wow," said Maggie. "It must be really great to be in on an a big discovery like that. I wonder if your dad's team will be able to solve the mystery of how the styracosaurus died."

Fenton looked at Willy. He hadn't planned on telling anyone about finding the claw until he had a chance to show it to the paleontologists, but somehow he had the feeling that Maggie would really appreciate it.

"Actually," he said, grinning, "Willy and I may have discovered a pretty important clue. You see, we were out there digging after everyone went home the other day, and we uncovered something kind of interesting."

"Fenton thinks it's a claw," said Willy excitedly.

"A claw?" asked Maggie. "From what?"

"Well, I can't be absolutely positive," said Fenton, "but it looks a lot to me like it's from some sort of dromaeosaurid."

"Wow!" said Maggie. "You mean like a velociraptor?"

"Something related to one," said Fenton. "All the dromaeosaurids had these big curved claws on the second toes of their back feet."

"Right," said Maggie. "I remember." Her eyes widened. "So what do you think the claw means?"

"I don't know," said Fenton. "It sure seems like the styracosaurus didn't die alone. *Something* must have killed both of those dinosaurs together. We'll have to show it to my father and the others."

"You mean they haven't seen it yet?" asked Maggie.

"Well, we only found it yesterday," said Fenton. "I was going to ride back out to the dig site today after school and show it to them, but I thought we should probably meet to talk about our project first."

"Okay," said Maggie. "So what are we waiting for? We've talked about it, and we know just what we're doing. Let's ride out to the dig site."

Fenton looked at his watch. "It's already after five. The team will be coming back down the mountain soon." He thought a moment. "I've got an idea, though. Let's all three meet after school tomorrow and ride up there together."

"Great," said Maggie, her green eyes shining.

6

"I don't understand it," said Fenton as the three of them stood in the trailer at the dig site the following afternoon. "It was right here." He looked in the yellow bin again, but it was empty except for a package of index cards and a few paper clips. "Willy, you were here when I brought it inside."

"I definitely saw you bring it into the trailer with the tools," said Willy. "Are you sure that's where you put it?"

"Positive," said Fenton. "I wrapped it up in my bandanna and put it in this box."

"Maybe it's in one of the other yellow boxes on that shelf," suggested Maggie.

Fenton checked the rest of the yellow bins. There was quite a collection of stuff—balls of string, rubber bands, somebody's sunglasses, a first-aid kit, a bottle opener—but no claw anywhere in sight. He couldn't believe it.

Just then Lily Martin walked into the trailer.

"Oh, hello," she said. "I had no idea you kids were even here."

71

"Hi, Professor Martin," said Fenton. "You know Willy, and this is my friend Maggie."

"Nice to meet you," said Professor Martin.

"Hi," said Maggie.

"We were just looking for something, Professor Martin," said Fenton. "Do you know if anyone took anything out of one of these yellow plastic boxes on the shelf?"

"What kind of thing?" asked Professor Martin.

"Well," said Fenton, looking at Willy and Maggie, "it was sort of going to be a surprise. But it was wrapped in a blue bandanna."

"I haven't seen anything like that," said Professor Martin. "Why don't you go ask your father and Charlie? They're over by the excavation site."

"Okay," said Fenton. That must be the explanation; his father or Charlie must have gone into the bin for something and discovered the claw already. Why, they probably had it right now.

Fenton, Maggie, and Willy found Charlie and Mr. Rumplemayer standing by the rock formation, looking over some newly excavated fossils. Fenton glanced quickly around, but there was no claw in sight.

"Dad, Charlie," he said quickly, starting to feel kind of worried, "did either of you take something out of the yellow boxes in the trailer?"

"Well, hello to you, too," joked his father.

"Sorry," said Fenton. "It's just that I left something really important in there, and now it's gone."

"It was wrapped in a blue bandanna," added Willy.

"Sounds pretty mysterious," said Charlie. He smiled at Maggie. "Howdy do? I'm Charlie."

"Hi," she answered. "My name's Maggie."

"Son," said Fenton's father, "where are your manners today?"

"Sorry," said Fenton again. "It's just that I really have to find this thing."

"Well, I haven't seen anything wrapped in a blue bandanna," said Mr. Rumplemayer. "What is it you're missing?"

Fenton looked dejectedly at Maggie and Willy.

"Well," he began, "I was saving it to be a surprise. Remember the other day, when Willy and I stayed late to work on that fossil?"

"Sure," said Mr. Rumplemayer.

"Two dedicated dino-diggers, if you ask me," said Charlie, smiling.

"Well, I think we found something really important," said Fenton. "A claw."

"A claw?" repeated his father.

"Yeah," said Willy excitedly. "From a drama—, a drama—"

"It was from some kind of a dromaeosaurid," said Fenton.

"Really?" said Mr. Rumplemayer. "Are you sure?"

"Positive," said Fenton.

73

"But then why didn't you tell me about it when you got home?" asked Fenton's father.

"Like I said, I was saving it to be a surprise," said Fenton. "I wanted to come out here and show it to you myself."

"I don't know, Fenton," said his father. "Are you absolutely certain that it was a dromaeosaurid claw? It doesn't make much sense, really, since all the other fossils we've found have been from a styracosaurus."

"I told you, I'm *positive*," said Fenton. "However the styracosaurus died, it wasn't alone. Don't you see, whatever killed the styracosaurus probably killed the dromaeosaurid, too, Dad!"

"Well," said Fenton's father. "It sounds like a very interesting find, but the fact is the claw doesn't seem to be anywhere in sight."

Fenton hung his head. Unfortunately, what his father was saying was right.

7

Over the weekend, as Fenton, Maggie, and Willy worked on the project for the Dinosaur Fair, Fenton couldn't get the missing claw out of his mind. Maggie brought over the chicken bones, and the three of them spent hours picking the meat off them and boiling them clean on Saturday. On Sunday, they mixed up some of the plaster Fenton had gotten from Ms. Schell and began to construct the model rock formations that would conceal the bones. The more they worked on the project, the more certain Fenton became that they were going to win one of the prizes at the Fair. They were so busy that he didn't have time to ride out and visit the dig site at all, and he almost forgot to contact Max for Treasure Quest on Saturday night. Through it all, though, he kept thinking about the missing claw. There just didn't seem to be any explanation for its disappearance.

On Monday afternoon in science, Mrs. Rigby asked the class how they were doing with their projects.

"The Dinosaur Fair is only a week away," she said. "So your projects should all be well on their way by now. Now, is anyone having any problems with what they're working on? Are there any questions?"

Peter raised his hand.

"Well," he said, "Franklin and my project is going okay, but we are having one little problem with our iguanodon."

"What's wrong?" cracked Buster from the back of the room. "Can't you find a cage big enough to keep it in?"

Mrs. Rigby gave him a sharp look. "Now, what seems to be the problem, Peter?"

"Well," Peter said. "It's just that we're not really sure about the way iguanodon stood."

"I mean, we know it could stand on its two back feet," said Franklin, "but some books show it with its back up straight, sort of like a kangaroo, and other books show it more bent over, with its front feet closer to the ground. Which one is right?"

"That's a very good question," said Mrs. Rigby. "The bent-over posture is generally thought to be more accurate." She looked at Fenton. "Fenton, I believe there's an iguanodon skeleton in the collection of the New York Museum of Natural History. Have you seen it?"

Fenton nodded. "It's bent over, like you said, with its tail sticking straight out behind it. But it wasn't always that way."

"Oh?" said Mrs. Rigby, looking interested.

"Yeah," said Fenton. "When the museum first got the skeleton a long time ago, it was missing the tail, and they set up the rest of the dinosaur straight up and down, like a kangaroo. Then later, when they got the tail, they realized that the iguanodon could never have stood like that, with its tail pointed down, without breaking its tail somewhere in the middle. So they changed the whole thing to the way it is now."

"Is that so?" said Mrs. Rigby. "That's fascinating, Fenton. But where was the missing tail to begin with?"

"Well, the skeleton was first dug up by these two brothers who got into a big fight about which one of them had found it first," said Fenton. "So one night, while one brother was sleeping, the other brother and some members of the dig crew started to steal the skeleton. They had only managed to get away with the tail when the rest of the camp woke up. So one brother had the body, and the other brother had the tail."

"Really!" said Mrs. Rigby. "Imagine!"

Lisa raised her hand.

"What did the thieves do with the tail?" she asked.

"They sold it to a collector," said Fenton.

"So how did they get the tail back, Fen?" asked Maggie.

"One of the crew members who had been hired to steal it started to feel bad about it, so he reported it to the museum," explained Fenton.

"Isn't that an interesting story?" said Mrs. Rigby. "Well, I guess that answers your question, Peter and Franklin. Now, does anyone else have any questions?"

"Yeah," said Buster loudly. "I have one. What did they do to the guy who squealed?"

"Um, excuse me?" said Fenton, twisting in his seat to look at Buster.

"What did the brother who took the tail do to the guy who turned him in?" said Buster. "I mean, nobody likes a fink. I bet he wanted to kill that rat."

"Uh, I'm not sure," said Fenton. "I mean, I never really heard that part of the story."

"I'll bet." Buster glared at him. "You know, it looks to me like maybe you're not so clever after all, Oddball."

"Huh?" said Fenton.

"Buster," said Mrs. Rigby, "that's it. I've warned you before about your rude attitude, and I've had enough. I'm giving you your fourth demerit. Report to Miss Stein in the library this afternoon for detention."

Fenton sunk down in his seat. Great, he thought. Now Buster will probably blame me for his detention and hate me more than ever. He glanced quickly over at Maggie, who rolled her eyes.

"Jerk," she mouthed silently.

Fenton nodded slightly.

"Creep," he managed to mouth back.

78

Later, as he, Maggie, and Willy were riding their bikes up the road toward home, Fenton thought of something.

"Hey," he called to the others, "do we have any plaster left?"

"Good question," said Maggie, stopping her bike.

"I think we're just about out," said Willy, pulling up beside them. "I wonder if Ms. Schell's still in the art room."

Fenton looked at his watch. Three-twenty. "Maybe I can catch her if I ride back really fast," he said. He took off his backpack and threw it by the side of the road. "Willy, you stay here and watch my stuff, okay? Then Maggie can go home and take care of Pepper."

"Okay, sounds good," said Maggie, pushing off on her bike. "See you at your place later."

"I'll be right here," called Willy.

Fenton took off on his bike as fast as he could, and in a little over ten minutes he was back at school. He leaned his bike against the bike rack and ran across the school yard, back into the building.

Luckily, Ms. Schell was still in the art room, cleaning up from her last class.

"Oh, Fenton," she said, looking up with a smile, "hello."

"Hi, Ms. Schell," said Fenton, panting. "Listen, I was wondering. Do you think I could have some more of that plaster?"

"My goodness, have you already used up what I gave you?" she asked.

"Well, it's kind of a big project," he said.

"Certainly you can have some more," said Ms. Schell. "It's in the supply cabinet. Help yourself."

Fenton took a medium-sized bag of plaster from the supply cabinet and tucked it under his arm.

"Thanks a lot, Ms. Schell!" he called as he left the room.

Making his way down the hall, Fenton thought about how strange it felt to be in the building after school hours. The halls were usually crowded with kids, but now there was no one in sight.

As he rounded a corner of the hall to head toward the exit, someone suddenly stepped out in front of him, blocking his path.

It was Buster.

"B-Buster, hi," said Fenton, startled. "What are you doing here?"

"Very funny," said Buster, chewing menacingly on a wad of gum.

"Oh, right," said Fenton, feeling his face flush. Buster must have just come from detention.

"Listen here, Oddball," said Buster, cracking his gum. "I just want you to know that I'm onto your little trick, and I don't think it's a very smart idea."

"Huh?" said Fenton.

"Believe me," said Buster. "If you keep it up, I can make your life at this school very unpleasant."

80

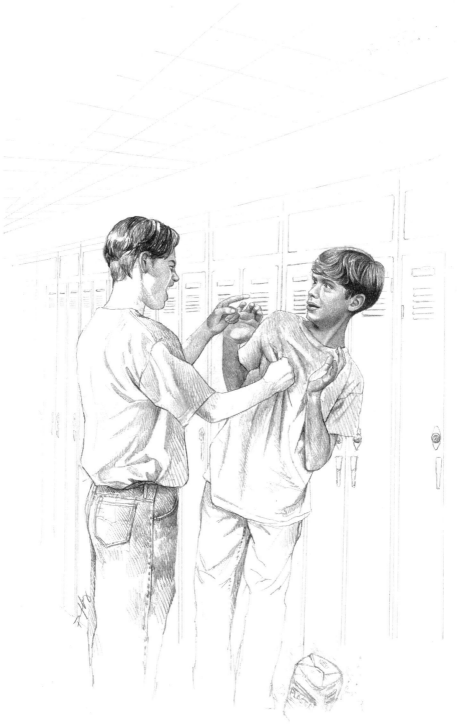

"Buster, if it's about detention—" Fenton began, shifting the bag of plaster to his other arm.

"Stop trying to be cute, Oddball. You know what I'm talking about," said Buster.

"No, I don't," said Fenton. "I have no idea what you mean."

"You know just what I mean," said Buster, taking a step closer to Fenton. "I know you think you're pretty smart. But if you keep it up, you're going to find out just how stupid you really are."

"Buster, really," said Fenton, looking nervously up and down the hall. "I don't know what you're talking about." Why didn't someone walk by? he thought. A teacher, anyone.

"Just consider this a warning," said Buster, taking another step closer to Fenton and poking him once in the chest with a finger. "Knock off all the cute comments in class, or you're going to be sorry you ever came to this school."

He broke into one of his evil grins and blew a big black bubble with his gum.

"See you later, Oddball," he said, turning and walking away.

At first Fenton just stood there, looking at the empty space where Buster had been standing. He was shaking a little, and for a moment his legs wouldn't move.

Then he turned and ran out the door to the school yard as fast as he could.

8

"What do you think it was all about?" asked Willy as the three of them sat in Fenton's kitchen later that afternoon.

"I have no idea," said Fenton, shaking his head.

"It sure is weird, Fen," said Maggie.

"I bet he was probably just mad at you because he had to go to detention," said Willy.

"Yeah," said Fenton. "I guess you're right. Come on, let's just get to work on the project and try to forget about it."

"Can we make lemonade first?" asked Maggie.

"I don't know if we have any lemons," said Fenton.

"No problem," said Maggie, reaching into her backpack and pulling out a bag of lemons.

"Maggie, you brought those from home?" asked Fenton.

"Yeah," she said, grinning. "It was really funny. Of course as soon as I walked into the kitchen Dina asked me what I wanted to eat. So I looked at her with a completely straight face and told her I was really in the mood for about ten lemons. You should have seen her expression—between the lemons and the chicken bones, she's beginning to think I'm nuts!"

They all laughed.

On Friday in homeroom, Maggie and Fenton sat at their desks while Mrs. Rigby called the roll.

"Adams, Marnie."

"Here!"

"Barretto, David."

"Here!"

Just then the door to the classroom opened and Matt Lewis walked in.

"Uh, I guess I'm late," he said, looking around sheepishly.

"I'm afraid the bell has already rung, Matt, which means I'm going to have to give you a demerit," said Mrs. Rigby, making a mark in her book.

"Finally!" said Buster from the back of the room. "It's about time someone else got a demerit around here."

Mrs. Rigby looked at him sternly.

"Buster, it seems to me that the last thing you should be doing now is working toward another afternoon of detention," she said. "Now kindly keep your thoughts to yourself while I finish calling the roll."

As Mrs. Rigby went on calling out the names and Matt

made his way through the rows of desks to his seat, Fenton noticed something.

"Hey, look at that," he whispered to Maggie.

"What?" Maggie whispered back.

"Matt," said Fenton, jerking his head toward the back of the room. "Did you notice anything weird?"

Maggie craned her neck to see.

"What do you mean?" she asked.

"I hear talking," said Mrs. Rigby, looking up from her roll book. "Whoever it is, please be quiet."

She went back to calling the roll. Fenton waited until her eyes were pointed down at her book.

"*Matt* was carrying Buster's backpack," he whispered to Maggie.

"Are you sure? Why would he?" asked Maggie. "They didn't even come to school together."

"I'm positive," said Fenton. "It was yellow and it had the same purple stain on it. No two backpacks could look that much alike."

"Then it must not be Buster's backpack after all," said Maggie. "It's got to be Matt's."

"But then why did Buster have it last week on the bus?" asked Fenton.

"I hear talking again," said Mrs. Rigby, sounding angry. Her eyes scanned Maggie and Fenton's row. "I hope I don't have to spend the morning giving out demerits. Now, let's see if we can finish this roll call without further interruption."

Silently Maggie looked at Fenton and put a finger to her lips. Fenton nodded. He knew there was no point in their starting to collect demerits; the last thing either of them wanted was to have to spend an afternoon in detention with Buster.

That afternoon Fenton, Willy, and Maggie rode up Sleeping Bear Mountain to try to find the missing claw.

As they approached the dig site, Fenton could see his father and Charlie.

"Hi, Dad!" Fenton called, laying his bike on the ground and walking toward the trailer.

"Hello, kids," said Mr. Rumplemayer. "I'm surprised to see you three up here. I thought you were spending all your free time working on your project for the fair."

"Well, we're practically finished," said Fenton.

"Yeah," said Maggie. "We decided to take a break and come up here for a little while."

"We're taking a little break ourselves," said Mr. Rumplemayer.

"Where's Professor Martin?" asked Maggie.

"Oh, she's digging," said Charlie. "She said she thought she might be working on something interesting."

"By the way, Fenton," said Mr. Rumplemayer, "we got a very nice letter from your teacher thanking us for the class visit and inviting us all to attend the science fair on Monday as special guests."

"That's great," said Fenton. "Are you coming?"

"Sure," said his father. "We all are."

"Oh good," said Willy. "Then you'll get to see the project for yourselves."

"Wouldn't miss it for the world," said Charlie. "I remember the science fair well. The highlight of the year, if you ask me."

"You've been to it before?" asked Fenton.

"Been to it? I had a prize-winning project!" boomed Charlie. "A map of the earthquake fault lines of the United States—best project in the whole Earth Sciences Fair, I thought. But my partner and I only won second place. Maxine Maxwell and Rusty Carmichael won first prize with their model of an exploding volcano. All showy stuff, it was; nothing to it, really."

"Wait a minute, Charlie," said Fenton. "*You* went to Morgan Elementary?"

"Sure," said Charlie.

Fenton was amazed. "How come you never told me that before?"

Charlie thought a moment. "Gee, I don't know, Fenton," he said. "I guess because you never asked me." He laughed and reached into his pants pocket to pull out a pack of gum.

"Wow, Charlie, is that Bubble Blasters?" asked Fenton excitedly.

"Afraid not," said Charlie. "I seem to have lost my pack of

Bubble Blasters somewhere. Can't exactly figure out how. You're welcome to a stick of regular old spearmint, though."

"No thanks, Charlie, that's okay," said Fenton. He had really been looking forward to trying another one of the Bubble Blasters' unusual flavors.

Just then there was a yell from over at the fossil site.

"Oh my goodness! Hurry! Hurry! Come quickly!"

Charlie stood up.

"Come on," he said, looking at the others. "It's Professor Martin!"

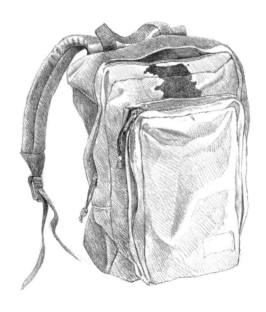

9

"Oh, I hope I didn't startle you all," said Professor Martin. "It's just that I've discovered something astounding."

"What is it?" asked Fenton.

"It's a bone," she said. "And it's definitely not from a styracosaurus. Come and see for yourselves."

She led the group over to where she had been working.

"Look at that," she said, indicating a six-inch-long bone imbedded in the rock.

"It's beautifully preserved," commented Fenton's father.

"Looks like an ulna," said Charlie.

"Yes," said Professor Martin. "I'm pretty sure it is."

Fenton bent down to examine the ulna, a bone from the forearm. It was long and thin, almost delicate. He agreed—it couldn't possibly be from a styracosaurus. The horned dinosaurs all had strong, stout, powerfully built front legs.

As far as Fenton was concerned, there was no doubt at all what kind of dinosaur it was from.

"A dromaeosaurid!" he said excitedly.

"Oh my gosh, Fenton, you were right!" said Maggie.

"Wow," said Willy.

"Yes, some sort of dromaeosaurid is my guess too," said Professor Martin.

"But I'm not guessing," said Fenton. "Didn't my father tell you, Professor Martin? I found a dromaeosaurid claw up here last week."

"He did mention that you said you had found something that you thought was a claw," said Professor Martin, "but that it had somehow mysteriously disappeared."

"I *knew* it was a dromaeosaurid claw," said Fenton dejectedly, wondering for what felt like the millionth time how the fossil could have just vanished like that.

"Well, there's definitely no doubt that there are parts of at least two dinosaurs buried here," said Mr. Rumplemayer. "You are right about that."

"But how come they died together?" asked Fenton.

"We can't tell for sure, but maybe there was a flood. Or maybe they didn't die together at all. It could be that they died separately, near the same river."

But Fenton was sure something more interesting than that had happened, and he was determined to find the claw and prove it.

10

Riding down the mountain was always a lot easier than riding up, thought Fenton as he, Maggie, and Willy coasted down Sleeping Bear Mountain Road. His stomach growled, and he wondered what there was back at the house to snack on before dinner. Hadn't he seen a jar of peanut butter in the refrigerator when he took out the milk for his cereal this morning? Maybe there were some crackers or something somewhere too.

Peanut butter, that was one of the flavors of Charlie's Bubble Blasters gum, wasn't it? Fenton had kind of wanted to try that one. Too bad Charlie's pack had disappeared like that; it would have been fun to watch Maggie's and Willy's faces as they bit into a piece of root-beer or licorice gum.

Wait a minute, thought Fenton, suddenly realizing something. The thought grew, and before he knew it, his bicycle had screeched to a halt on the side of the road.

"That's it!" he said out loud.

"Fenton, what happened?" asked Willy, circling back around to where Fenton had stopped.

"Are you okay?" asked Maggie, pulling up beside them. "Why did you stop like that? Do you have another flat or something?"

"Licorice!" declared Fenton, still thinking.

"Fen, what are you talking about?" asked Maggie.

"Really," said Willy. "What about licorice?"

"That day Buster threatened me in the hall after school," said Fenton. "He was chewing gum."

"So?" asked Willy.

"It was black gum," said Fenton. "I saw it when he blew a bubble."

"Black gum, that's weird," said Maggie.

"It sure is," said Fenton. "A little too weird, if you ask me."

"Fenton, this is really fascinating," said Willy, "but can't it wait till we get back home? It's hot out here."

"Just listen, Willy," said Fenton excitedly. "Back there at the dig site, when I asked Charlie about his gum, he said he lost his pack of Bubble Blasters, right?"

"Right," said Maggie. "So . . ."

"So, Bubble Blasters is this really unusual chewing gum that comes in all these weird flavors, like popcorn and marshmallow and caramel—"

"And licorice?" said Willy, his eyes widening.

"And licorice," said Fenton, nodding.

92

"Do you think Buster *stole* Charlie's gum?" asked Willy.

"Wait a minute, let's be logical," said Maggie. "After all, Buster could have just had his own pack of Bubble Blasters, couldn't he?"

"But that's just it," said Fenton. "Charlie said you can't get Bubble Blasters anywhere around here. He has a friend send it to him from California."

"*I've* never seen licorice gum in any of the stores in Morgan," said Willy.

"Neither have I," agreed Maggie. "Wow, so Buster probably did take it. He could have done it that day when the class went to the dig site."

"That's what I think," said Fenton. "Charlie kept his gum in a bin in the trailer. Buster probably took it while everyone was looking at Professor Martin's drawings."

"Hey, remember when Mrs. Rigby yelled at Buster on the bus?" said Maggie suddenly. "It was because he was chewing gum!"

"Oh, yeah," said Fenton. "I bet it was Charlie's Bubble Blasters."

"Wow," said Willy, shaking his head. "Stealing something on a class trip; that sounds like something Buster would do."

Fenton stared at him.

"Willy, you're absolutely right!" he said suddenly, his mind racing. He turned to Maggie. "Who's Buster's partner for the Dinosaur Fair?" he asked.

"Matt," she answered. "Buster got paired with Matt, I think, and Jen and Jason got put together. What's this all about, Fen?"

"I'm not completely sure yet myself," said Fenton. "But I think I know how we can find out. Willy, where do you think Buster would keep something if he didn't want anyone to find out about it?"

"Easy," said Willy. "The clubhouse at the lumberyard."

"That's what I think too," said Fenton. "And the way I see it, there's only one thing for us to do now."

"What's that?" asked Maggie.

Fenton looked at them. "I think it's time we took a good look around that clubhouse."

"What?" cried Willy. "You must be crazy, Fenton!"

"Really," said Maggie. "Buster's never going to let us near his clubhouse."

"Well then, we'll have to go sometime when he won't notice us as easily," said Fenton. "Like at night."

"Forget it, Fen," said Maggie. "If you think I'm going to go snooping around Buster's clubhouse in the dark just because of some bubble gum, think again."

"But that's just it, you guys," said Fenton. "I'm beginning to think there's a whole lot more to this than just a pack of gum."

11

"So Maggie's sister is going to drive you boys back home after the movie too, right?" asked Fenton's father later that evening.

Fenton glanced at Willy, who was sitting next to him on the couch.

"Uh, yes, Dad," he said. "That's right. She and her boyfriend are going to pick us up and drop us off."

"They're going to the movie too," added Willy.

"All right," said Mr. Rumplemayer. "Just make sure they bring you all the way up to the house. It'll be dark, so don't let them drop you down at the turnoff."

"Okay," said Fenton, patting the flashlight in his jean-jacket pocket. He felt kind of bad that he hadn't exactly told his father all of their plans for that night, but after all, he hadn't lied to him either. He, Maggie, and Willy *were* going to the movies in town with Maggie's older sister Lila and Lila's boyfriend. He just hadn't mentioned the fact that they had decided to go because the movie theater was just down the street from the lumberyard. Or that they planned to cut out after the movie began to do a little snooping around Buster's clubhouse.

It was Maggie who had thought of the movie idea. Lila and her boyfriend went every Friday night, she said. All Maggie had to do was tell her mother that she and her friends wanted to go too, and Lila would have to take them. Mrs. Carr thought Lila and Maggie should spend more time together; she just didn't seem to understand that her two daughters had practically nothing in common.

A pair of headlights swept the far wall of the living room as a car drove into the driveway and honked its horn twice.

"That must be them," said Fenton, jumping up. "Bye, Dad, see you later."

"Bye, Mr. Rumplemayer," said Willy, hurrying after him.

A red convertible was parked in the driveway, its motor running. Maggie waved at them from the backseat.

"Hi," she said as Fenton and Willy climbed in beside her. She pointed to the older girl and boy in the front seat. "That's Lila and Rob. Lila, these are my friends."

"Pleasure," said Lila sounding bored and flipping her auburn hair over her shoulder as Rob stepped on the gas.

96

"I still don't get this, Maggie," whispered Fenton as the car took off down the dirt road. "Isn't it going to be a little hard for us to sneak out of the movie theater with your sister and her boyfriend there?"

"Don't worry about them," said Maggie, waving her hand toward the front seat as if she were brushing away a fly. "They care even less about us than we do about them. Watch—they won't even want to sit with us."

A few minutes later they arrived at the Morgan Cinema. Maggie was right about Lila and Rob; they bought their tickets and made their way into the theater ahead of Maggie, Fenton, and Willy without so much as a backward glance.

"Make sure you keep your ticket stubs so we can get back in," said Maggie.

"Good thinking," said Fenton. "And let's sit in the back so we can sneak out easily after the movie starts."

"I want some popcorn," said Willy.

"Why?" asked Fenton, taking a seat near the aisle. "We're not staying."

Willy shrugged.

"I'm hungry," he said, making his way back out toward the lobby.

A few minutes later Willy was back with his popcorn, and the lights of the theater began to dim. The movie was called *S.O.S. Earth*, and it was about creatures from another planet trying to take over the earth. It looked pretty good, and if he, Maggie, and Willy hadn't had such an important mission to take care of that night, Fenton definitely would have wanted to stay and see it.

He turned to Maggie and Willy as a bunch of spaceships were landing in a field behind an old man's house.

"Now?" he whispered.

"Now," Maggie whispered back, nodding.

They crept back up the aisle and out through the lobby of the theater.

"Gee, it's kind of dark down there," said Willy, munching on his popcorn as he peered down the road toward the lumberyard.

"Good thing I brought this," said Fenton, taking the flashlight out of his pocket and turning it on.

They walked down the dark, deserted street, following the tiny beam of the flashlight. As they approached the Wadsworth Museum, Fenton noticed a light glowing in a rear window. He thought of Mrs. Wadsworth sitting in the little room in the back where she lived, probably cleaning some new specimen to put on display.

"There it is," said Willy as they approached the lumberyard. "That little building in the back is the clubhouse."

"It looks like someone's there," said Maggie, pointing toward the glowing windows of the little building. "We'd better be careful."

They crept around the side of the larger building and began to make their way past a fenced-in yard with two pickup trucks and several stacks of lumber inside.

Suddenly Fenton heard a low growl from the other side of the fence.

"What was that?" asked Willy.

Fenton turned the beam of the flashlight toward the sound. "Oh, no," he said.

Crouched in front of them, directly on the other side of the fence, was a huge dog, baring its teeth.

"Now what do we do?" asked Maggie, as the three of them froze in place.

"Nice doggie, nice doggie," said Willy quietly. He reached into his bucket and tossed the rest of his popcorn through the fence.

They all waited as the dog sniffed the kernels on the ground.

Fenton let out a deep breath as the dog began to gobble the popcorn and wag its tail. "Come on," he whispered, shining the flashlight beam on the ground.

As quietly as they could, they made their way to the little building in the back. The clubhouse was really just an old storage shed, as Willy had said. The small, grimy windows glowed with dim light, and Fenton could hear muffled voices from inside. Someone was definitely there.

Fenton shone the beam of his flashlight on the old, wooden

door. Nailed to the front of it was a messy, hand-painted sign that said PRIVATE—KEEP OUT—THIS MEANS YOU!

"Come on," whispered Fenton, creeping around the side of the building. "Let's try to take a look through the windows."

"They're too high," whispered Maggie, straining up on tiptoe to reach a window. "We'll never see over the sill."

"There must be something around here we can stand on," said Fenton, looking around.

"How about that over there?" whispered Willy, pointing at an old wooden crate that was filled with empty cans.

"Perfect," said Fenton. "Help me empty it out so we can move it."

Fenton held the flashlight under one arm, and he, Maggie, and Willy removed the cans one by one and put them on the ground, being careful not to let them knock against each other. They positioned the crate directly under the window, and Fenton turned off the flashlight, putting it back in his pocket. The three of them squeezed together and climbed onto the crate.

"What do you see?" whispered Willy, squirming to position himself.

Fenton reached into his back pocket and pulled out a purple bandanna. He gently rubbed the dirt away from a portion of the window, put the bandanna on the windowsill, and peered through the glass.

The room inside was filled with pieces of old furniture and was littered with empty soda cans and candy wrappers. At the far corner was a rickety-looking card table, and right near it were Buster and Matt.

"Oh my gosh," whispered Maggie.

Buster put a bottle of glue down on the table and wiped his hands with a blue-and-white rag.

Fenton's eyes traveled to the table, and he felt a shiver go through his body. So he had been right after all.

"Look," he whispered. "Look at what's on top of the table."

"What *is* that?" asked Maggie.

"Well, I can't be sure," whispered Fenton, "but I'd say it's pretty likely that what we're looking at now is Buster's project for the Dinosaur Fair."

Sitting on top of the table was a wooden box turned upside down to serve as a small platform. Painted on the front of the box, in the same messy scrawl as the sign on the clubhouse door, were the words AMAZING NEW MINIATURE HORNED DINOSAUR SKULL, DISCOVERED BY BUSTER CREGG. In smaller letters underneath it said DISPLAY STAND MADE BY BUSTER CREGG AND MATT LEWIS.

On top of the platform was the skull of an animal. It was about four inches long and had a narrow, pointy shape. But the astonishing thing about it was the fierce-looking curved horn growing out of its forehead.

"What is that?" asked Willy.

"It's not really a dinosaur, is it, Fen?" asked Maggie. "I mean, it doesn't look like any dinosaur I've ever seen."

"Is it really an amazing new discovery?" asked Willy. "Where did Buster find it?"

"No, it's definitely not a dinosaur," said Fenton. "In fact, I'd say it looks a lot like a lizard of some sort."

"It looks kind of like an iguana," said Maggie.

Fenton and Willy looked at each other.

"Mrs. Wadsworth!" they both said at once.

"Mrs. Wadsworth told us she was missing an iguana skull," Fenton explained to Maggie. "She left it out in front of the museum to bleach, and it disappeared. Buster must have seen it there and taken it."

"Wait a minute, though, Fen," said Maggie. "What about that horn? Iguanas don't have horns. In fact, I've never heard of any lizard with one."

"Then maybe it *is* a dinosaur," said Willy.

"It is definitely not a dinosaur," said Fenton again. "And I have news for you—that pointy thing isn't a horn either, although Buster obviously thinks it is."

"Then what is it?" asked Maggie.

"It's a claw," said Fenton. "A dromaeosaurid claw."

"Oh, wow," said Willy.

"And that blue rag Buster's wiping his hands on is my bandanna, the one I wrapped the claw in the day I found it."

Maggie gasped.

"That's right," said Fenton. "It looks like Charlie's gum wasn't the only thing that Buster took that day at the dig site."

Fenton shifted on the box to get a better look and suddenly began to lose his footing.

"Oh, no," he said, reaching out to grab on to Willy and Maggie. But the crate was slipping out from under them, and before he knew it, they had all fallen to the ground, landing on the loose cans with a loud clatter.

"Hey, what's that?" they heard Buster yell from inside as the dog began barking furiously behind them.

"Watch out!" said Maggie, scrambling to get up. "He's coming!"

"What if he sees us?" said Willy.

"Come on, quick!" said Fenton as they all began to run. "Let's get out of here!"

12

"Whew, that was close!" said Willy as the three of them stood panting in front of the Morgan Cinema.

"But worth it," said Maggie. "At least we managed to solve the mystery of the claw."

"Buster heard my father and the others talking about the styracosaurus that day at the dig site, so when he found the claw in the trailer, he probably thought it was a horn," said Fenton.

"And he figured a project with a genuine dinosaur horn glued on to it was bound to win him a prize," said Willy.

"So now what do we do?" asked Maggie.

"We should probably tell your father, right?" asked Willy.

"I'm not so sure," said Fenton. After all, the claw had been his discovery in the first place. Now he really wanted to be the one to get it back. "Maybe we can think of a plan on our own."

"Like what?" asked Maggie.

"I don't know yet," said Fenton. "But I bet we can come up

with something. We have to get the skull and the claw back." He looked at his watch. "But right now we better get back inside the theater before the movie ends."

The following afternoon, the three of them sat up in Fenton's room, working on the project and trying to figure out what they should do about Buster.

"We can't let him get away with this," said Maggie, carefully sculpting a plaster rock formation around a chicken thighbone.

"Really," said Willy. "I can't believe Buster—that thief!"

"That's for sure," said Fenton. "We caught him red-handed: All the evidence was right there—the skull, the claw, even my blue bandanna." Suddenly he thought of something. "Oh, no."

"What is it, Fen?" asked Maggie.

"My purple bandanna," said Fenton, remembering.

"I thought you said it was blue," said Willy.

"No, I mean, I had another bandanna with me last night, a purple one," said Fenton. "I used it to clean the window of the clubhouse, and I think I left it there when we ran off."

"Oops," said Willy. "I guess that means Buster'll probably find it there."

"If he hasn't already," said Maggie. "But hey, Buster doesn't have any way of knowing that it's *your* bandanna, Fen. All he knows for sure is that *someone* was snooping around his clubhouse."

That's true," said Fenton. "But I guess I'd better stop carrying bandannas around with me for a little while just to be safe."

"Good idea," said Willy.

"Meanwhile, what are we going to do about the skull and the claw?" asked Maggie. "We have to think of something."

"I know," said Fenton. "Buster definitely has to be stopped. Not only is he a thief, but he's cheating on his project, too. He thinks he can use a fake dinosaur to win a prize. Hey, that gives me an idea. . . ."

"What?" asked Willy.

"I just may have come up with a plan," said Fenton. "It's going to be hard, but if it works, we can get the claw back, keep Buster from showing his fake skull at the fair, and give him a pretty good scare, too." He grinned.

"What is it?" asked Willy and Maggie together.

Fenton looked at them.

"There's only one solution: We have to make a whole new project for the Dinosaur Fair," he said.

"Fen, you must be kidding!" said Maggie, holding up her plaster-covered hands. "What about all this?"

"We can't use it," said Fenton. "We have to scrap it and do something completely different."

"I don't get it," said Willy, shaking his head.

"Neither do I," said Maggie.

"Okay, well, listen," said Fenton. "Here's my idea. . . ."

107

13

"All right," said Fenton as he, Maggie, and Willy finished setting up their project on an easel in the gym on Monday, "I signed us up to be second. We present ours right after Peter and Franklin."

"When's Buster supposed to show his project?" asked Willy.

"He's going last," said Fenton. "Right before the judging. I walked over to his area to see what was going on, but he's got his project covered with a sheet for now. I guess he wants to make a big impression on the judges."

Maggie grinned. "If everything goes according to plan, he'll end up making a bigger impression than he knows."

Fenton looked around. Most of the other sixth graders were busy setting up their projects around the gym. The teachers and kids from the fourth and fifth grades, who had been invited to the fair, were milling around waiting for things to begin.

"Did you bring the note?" asked Willy.

Fenton patted his shirt pocket.

"It's right in here," he said.

"Hey, look," said Maggie. "There's your dad."

Fenton saw his father, Charlie, and Professor Martin make their way into the room and over toward Mrs. Rigby. To his relief, each of them wore a bandanna—Fenton's father and Charlie each had one tied around his neck, and Professor Martin had one around her straw hat.

"Hello, everyone," Mrs. Rigby began. "I'd like to welcome you all to this year's sixth-grade science fair—the Dinosaur Fair. First I'd like to introduce you to our special guests, the paleontologists who were kind enough to show the sixth grade around the Sleeping Bear Mountain dig site, Lily Martin, Charlie Smalls, and Bill Rumplemayer, father of our own Fenton."

There was some applause, and Fenton waved to his father, who waved back.

"Next I'd like you to welcome my fellow judges," she said. She gestured to the man and woman to her left. "Mr. Rafael, and Mrs. Soames, two of my fellow teachers who have agreed to help out."

There was some applause for the judges, and Mrs. Rigby went on.

"We have several projects to see today, so let's get started." She looked down at the list in her hand. "The first project presenters will be Peter Pomerantz and Franklin Lee."

"Over here, Mrs. Rigby!" called Peter.

Everyone made their way over to where Peter and Franklin were standing in front of a table. Fenton noticed Buster and his friends among the group of kids.

He turned to Willy.

"Now's probably a good time," he whispered. "Buster's coming over this way." He reached into his pocket and pulled out the note. "All the stuff is in my backpack under our easel."

Willy nodded and slipped away quietly.

Fenton saw his father and the other paleontologists heading toward him.

"Hello, son," said Mr. Rumplemayer. "Hello, Maggie. Where's Willy?"

"Oh, he had to do something," said Fenton. "He'll be back in a minute."

"So, when do we get to see this big project of yours?" asked Charlie, grinning.

"We're next," said Fenton, "but there've been a few changes in our project."

"It seems that way," said his father. "I was rather surprised that you left that big plaster-of-paris project you'd all been working so hard on at home."

"Oh, well," said Fenton. "We kind of had to change our idea."

"What do the bandannas have to do with it?" asked Professor Martin, patting her hat with one hand.

"Yeah, your dad told us that you had asked us to wear

110

them," said Charlie. "What's up?"

"Oh, they're kind of good luck," said Fenton, glancing at Maggie.

Just then Willy reappeared and gave Fenton the thumbs-up sign.

"Mission accomplished," he said.

"You did it?" whispered Fenton.

"Take a look," said Willy, jerking his thumb toward the other end of the room, where the judges' table was. There, tied to each of their chairs, was a bandanna.

"And you left the note for Buster?" asked Maggie.

"I put it and the shopping bag right by his project," said Willy.

"Nice work," said Fenton, grinning.

When everyone had assembled in front of the table, Peter and Franklin presented their project, which was all about the dinosaur iguanodon. They had several big, colorful charts showing where its bones had been found, how big it was, and what it ate. But the most impressive part of the project was the three-foot-tall model of iguanodon, in the bent-over posture, that they had made out of clay. It really was an amazing replica, Fenton had to admit. They had even somehow managed to make the dinosaur's skin look scaly, and they had painted it in an amazing combination of browns and golds.

"Pretty good, huh?" whispered Maggie.

"Yeah," said Fenton.

Everyone watching seemed impressed too. Everyone except Buster and his friends, who whispered throughout the presentation. Several times the whole gang burst out laughing, earning them a sharp look from Mrs. Rigby.

"Hey, you guys, you're up," said Willy as the other kids applauded Franklin and Peter's presentation.

"Next on our list," said Mrs. Rigby, looking down at her piece of paper, "are Maggie Carr and Fenton Rumplemayer. And it says here, 'With special help from Willy Whitefox.'"

"Good luck, son," said Mr. Rumplemayer.

"Yes, good luck," said Lily Martin.

"Break a leg, kids," said Charlie. "I mean, a fibula."

Fenton laughed.

"Here goes," he said to Maggie and Willy.

They led the judges and the rest of the crowd over to an easel against the opposite wall. Stacked on the easel were several large pieces of poster board, bound together with metal rings on the left side like a giant book. Painted on the cover of the book were the words BUNGLES AND BLUNDERS: TEN BIG MISTAKES IN DINOSAUR SCIENCE.

Fenton cleared his throat.

"Our project deals with some mistakes that have been made about dinosaurs in the past," he began.

"As we go through this book, we'll first show you the mistakes and then how they were corrected," said Maggie. She nodded at Willy, who took his place alongside the easel.

"The first dinosaur we are going to show you is hypsilophodon," said Fenton. "Hypsilophodon was a plant-eating dinosaur about six feet long." He looked at Willy, who flipped open the cover of the book to reveal a drawing of a hypsilophodon perched in a tree, its feet firmly grasping the branch beneath it.

"A man named Othenio Abel put together the bones of hypsilophodon in 1912," said Maggie. "Abel had the idea that the first toe on each of this dinosaur's hind feet was reversed—that it faced backward."

"Many people thought that hypsilophodon may have used this backward toe to hold on to the branches of trees, but it turned out that Abel had made a mistake. In fact, hypsilophodon's toes all pointed in the same direction—forward."

This time, when Willy flipped the page, it became apparent that the poster board had been cut horizontally, right above the dinosaur's feet. Willy turned only the bottom half of the page, so that the top half of the hypsilophodon remained in place. Now the bottom of the picture showed hypsilophodon's feet with all its toes facing the same way, standing firmly on the ground.

"We now know that hypsilophodon didn't live in trees at all," Fenton finished.

"The next big mistake we're going to show you has to do with iguanodon," said Maggie, signaling Willy to turn both halves of the page.

The picture on the following piece of poster board showed an iguanodon, its neck extended, its jaws closed, and a long, snakelike tongue protruding from a tiny hole at the front of its mouth.

"An early iguanodon fossil had a hole in the front of its jaw when it was found," she explained.

"Paleontologists thought that iguanodon might have had a long, narrow tongue that could poke out of this hole to search for leaves to eat," said Fenton. "Kind of like the way an anteater's tongue finds ants."

"But iguanodon fossils discovered later didn't have the hole in the jaw. It must have been just a small piece of bone that had somehow been chipped off," said Maggie. "We now know that iguanodon had to open its mouth to eat."

This time Willy flipped the top half of the page, so that only the part of the picture that showed the dinosaur's head changed. The new iguanodon head was opening its mouth to take a bite from the branch of a leafy tree.

Maggie and Fenton continued their presentation, with Willy flipping parts of the pages to illustrate the points. They talked about how the hadrosaurids, or duckbill dinosaurs, had once been thought to live underwater but were now known to be land dwellers. They explained that the plates on a stegosaurus's back had been called defensive armor, but were now thought to have more to do with raising and lowering the dinosaur's body temperature.

As the presentation went on, Fenton became aware of the intent looks on the faces of the other kids. The judges were all paying very close attention, and Mrs. Rigby had begun to take notes. It seemed like everyone was really interested in the project.

Everyone except Buster, that is. He and his friends continued to make faces, whisper, and giggle to each other throughout the presentation. It was all Fenton could do not to lose his concentration.

Just wait, thought Fenton. There'll be plenty of reason for Buster to start paying attention soon.

After he and Maggie had explained the drawings on the next few pieces of poster board, Fenton took a deep breath.

"And now," he said, glancing quickly first at Maggie and then at Willy, "we'd like to talk to you about some mistakes that have been made involving *dinosaur horns.*"

Suddenly Buster was looking at them. Jen went to whisper something in his ear, and he brushed her away.

We've got him, thought Fenton.

"Our first mistake was made by the famous dinosaur scientist Othniel Charles Marsh in 1887," said Maggie. "Marsh got ahold of some giant horns in Colorado and decided that they had belonged to an extinct buffalo."

Willy flipped the page to reveal a drawing of a large buffalo with huge, curved horns.

"But," said Fenton, "in 1888, similar horns, along with a

skull, were found on a ranch right here in Wyoming. This skull showed that the horns actually belonged to a dinosaur, which Marsh named triceratops."

Willy flipped the bottom half of the page so that the horns now sat on the head of a triceratops.

"Our next horned dinosaur mistake," said Fenton, glancing to make sure Buster was still paying attention, "is about something that turned out *not to be a horned dinosaur after all.*"

"That's right," said Maggie. "When the skeleton of iguanodon was first discovered in the 1850s, it was assembled with a spike-shaped horn on its nose."

Willy turned to the next drawing, which showed an iguanodon with a pointed piece on its snout.

"We now know that the spike-shaped piece was actually the dinosaur's thumb," said Maggie, glancing at Fenton and smiling as Willy flipped the top half of the page, replacing the portion of the picture that showed the dinosaur's head and hands.

"In fact," said Fenton, "the name iguanodon itself comes from an incorrect idea. Early dinosaur discoverers thought that dinosaurs were some type of giant lizard."

"But they're not," said Maggie. "They *are* related to other reptiles, but dinosaurs are their own group. The last part of our presentation has to do with some of the ways that dinosaurs are different from lizards."

Fenton sneaked a look at Buster, who had moved forward through the crowd and was paying closer attention than ever.

"Dinosaurs were once thought to crawl like lizards," he said, "with their legs sprawled out on either side of their bodies."

"But," said Maggie, "as our next picture shows, if a dinosaur such as diplodocus tried to walk with its legs like that, there wouldn't have been enough room underneath it for its belly."

Willy flipped the page to show a dinosaur, its legs sprawled out on either side of it and its stomach dragging on the ground, creating a deep ditch.

"We now know that dinosaurs walked with their legs tucked under them, the way elephants do," said Maggie.

"Finally," said Fenton, "there's one more very important difference between dinosaurs and lizards." He looked at Maggie and Willy and took a deep breath. "And that is, *they have completely different skulls.*"

Buster's mouth dropped open.

Willy flipped the page to a diagram of two skulls, and Fenton explained that dinosaur skulls have larger and more numerous holes in them than lizard skulls do.

"These holes made room for the big muscles in the dinosaur's head," said Maggie, "which allowed the dinosaur more strength than a lizard."

"So," said Fenton, raising his eyebrows, "now you all know how easy it is to tell a dinosaur skull from a lizard skull *at a single glance.*"

He looked at Buster, whose face had gone completely white. In fact, Buster looked like he was about to be sick.

"Thank you very much, Fenton, Maggie, and Willy," said Mrs. Rigby as the other kids burst into applause. "That was a very informative presentation. Now, our next presenters are Marnie Adams and Rebecca Stiles."

"Well, what do you think?" asked Maggie as the other kids moved away. "Did it work?"

"I think so," said Willy. "I was watching Buster the whole time, and he definitely started to look pretty worried."

"I saw it too," said Fenton. "I think we got to him."

"I bet he's on his way over to his project right now to count the holes in the skull," said Maggie, laughing.

"Let's just hope the second part of the plan works too," said Fenton.

The morning wore on, and the rest of the sixth graders presented their projects. Marnie and Rebecca did a report on the different theories of how and why the dinosaurs had become extinct. Ray and his partner displayed a game where the object was to guess whether a particular dinosaur was a carnivore—a meat eater—or an herbivore—a vegetarian. And Jason and Jen's project compared mythical creatures like dragons with actual dinosaurs.

But the most impressive project of all was David Barretto and Lisa's, a giant relief map of the earth. All the continents were movable, to demonstrate how they had once fit together like puzzle pieces but had eventually broken up and drifted apart. Lisa and David had even plotted the possible routes that dinosaurs had taken to travel across the continents. Fenton couldn't help thinking of the abandoned model-dig project and feeling a little jealous; it was obvious that Lisa and David had put a lot of time into their project. But Fenton knew that changing their own project was the only hope he, Maggie, and Willy had of recovering the claw and the skull peacefully.

"And now for our final project," said Mrs. Rigby, looking down at her list. "Buster Cregg and Matt Lewis." She looked around the room. "Buster, Matt?"

At first there was no answer. Then Matt spoke up.

"Um, I'm over here, Mrs. Rigby," he said. "But I don't know what happened to Buster."

"Well then, I guess you should just present your project on your own, Matt," said Mrs. Rigby.

"But I can't," he said.

"Why, what seems to be the problem?" asked Mrs. Rigby.

"Well," said Matt, "wherever Buster went, he must have taken our project with him."

Suddenly the room was filled with surprised murmurs.

"Well then, I suppose that means we've come to the end of our presentations," said Mrs. Rigby. "Everyone is dismissed to the school yard while we judges meet to discuss our decisions. We'll announce the prize winners back here in fifteen minutes."

"Come on," said Fenton, turning to Maggie and Willy. "That gives us just enough time to check the bike rack and see if the plan worked."

They rushed out of the gym, through the crowd of kids in the school yard, and over to the bike rack.

"There it is!" cried Maggie, pointing at the shopping bag on the ground.

Fenton picked up the bag and looked inside. There was the dromaeosaurid claw, the iguana skull, and even the rest of Charlie's Bubble Blasters, along with the note they had written and left for Buster. He pulled it out and read it again.

Wendell—We know what you're up to, and you can't get away with it. Don't even think about trying to show your phony project at the fair. This is your last chance to return everything you took. Put it all in this bag immediately and leave it near the bike rack if you don't want trouble.

— The Bandanna Band

He laughed, thinking of Buster and how he must have felt as he saw all those bandannas on the paleontologists and on the judges' chairs—especially if he had discovered the purple bandanna on his clubhouse windowsill.

121

"Well, I guess it worked," he said.

"It sure did," said Maggie gleefully.

"Now we can return the iguana skull to Mrs. Wadsworth," said Willy.

"That's right," said Fenton, pulling the claw out of the bag and turning it over in his hand. He stroked its smooth, curved surface, fingering the strange, small triangular chunk stuck to its pointed end. "And this can go back to its rightful skull."

Maggie looked at him. "*Skull*, Fen?"

Willy laughed. "Really, Fenton, you sound like you're starting to believe Buster's hoax. This claw isn't from a skull."

But Fenton was busy thinking. He turned the fossil over in his hand and examined the small, hard, triangular piece jammed onto the pointed end.

"Or *is* it?" he said. He looked at Maggie and Willy and grinned. "You guys, I think I just figured out how the styracosaurus died—and the dromaeosaurid, too!"

14

The following Saturday, Fenton, Maggie, Willy, Fenton's father, and Professor Martin sat by the trailer at the dig site while Charlie put some ribs on the barbecue nearby.

"Hope you're all hungry," said Charlie, brushing some of his homemade sauce on the ribs.

"Starved," said Fenton. He loved Charlie's barbecued ribs.

"Make sure you save room for dessert," said Professor Martin.

"Dessert?" asked Fenton's father.

"That's right," said Professor Martin. "I bought a nice big cake in town so we can have a real celebration."

"Well, there certainly is a whole lot to celebrate," said Charlie. "First Fenton, Maggie, and Willy win second prize for their dinosaur project, and then the dromaeosaurid claw shows up and turns out to be the key to the death of both dinosaurs."

"Sure was lucky," said Maggie, glancing at Fenton.

"I still don't understand where it disappeared to in the first place," said Charlie. "Or, for that matter, how my pack of chewing gum managed to reappear half empty." He narrowed his eyes and looked at Fenton, who shrugged.

"Well, the important thing is that the claw turned up," said Professor Martin. "Thanks to that claw, we've answered all the questions we had about how the styracosaurus died."

"Yes, you were absolutely right about that piece of bone near the tip, Fenton," said Mr. Rumplemayer. "It *was* from the styracosaurus skull."

"Wow," said Willy, "so the two dinosaurs *were* fighting, after all."

"Looks that way," said Charlie.

"What we think happened was that a group of dromaeosaurus dinosaurs called dromaeosauruses may have attacked the styracosaurus, probably somewhere near the banks of a river," said Professor Martin.

"And as they were kicking the larger dinosaur with their claws, one of them was unlucky enough to get his claw stuck in the styracosaurus's head," said Fenton's father.

"Pretty hard to balance with your foot stuck in someone else's head," said Charlie. "Or with someone else's foot stuck in *your* head, for that matter."

"Yeah," said Fenton. "So both the styracosaurus and the dromaeosaurus lost their balance and fell into the river."

"That seems to be what happened," said Fenton's father.

"The rest of the bones we found from both dinosaurs were completely jumbled. My guess is that they continued to struggle in the water and were washed downstream, eventually drowning together."

"Wow," said Willy. "What a cool story."

"The best part about it is that thanks to the piece of styracosaurus skull that was stuck on the end of the dromaeosaurus claw, we can pretty much figure out what positions the two animals were in when they died," said Mr. Rumplemayer. "And now that we have all that information, the museum has decided to mount the two skeletons exactly that way, as if they were in combat."

"That's great," said Fenton. He tried to imagine the display as it would look at the museum in New York, in the Hall of the Late Dinosaurs—the dromaeosaurus clutching on to the skull of the styracosaurus, and the styracosaurus throwing its head back, desperately trying to shake the predator off.

"All right," called Charlie, cutting into Fenton's thoughts. "Come and get it!"

Everyone lined up at the barbecue and Charlie dished out big helpings of ribs. Fenton, Maggie, and Willy took their plates to a rock a little ways away and sat down.

"Boy, it sure is a good thing we got that claw back," said Willy quietly.

"Really," said Maggie. "It's going to make the whole museum display possible."

"I bet Mrs. Wadsworth was pretty happy to find the skull on her front step too," said Fenton.

"Now maybe Buster will think twice before he takes stuff that doesn't belong to him," said Willy.

"He'll definitely reconsider before he cuts out of school again," said Maggie. "I can't believe Mrs. Rigby gave him a whole week of detention for that."

"It's too bad you guys couldn't show your original project," said Willy. "I bet you would have won first prize, no problem."

"I'm glad we switched, though," said Fenton. "If we hadn't done the new project, we probably never would have solved the mystery of how the styracosaurus died. Besides, David and Lisa's project was really good. They deserved to win."

"You know, there's one thing I never got to ask you, Fen," said Maggie, biting into a rib. "How did you know we would find the claw at Buster's clubhouse?"

"Really," said Willy. "How did you figure out that Buster took it?"

"Well," said Fenton, wiping the barbecue sauce off his mouth, "part of it was just a hunch. Somehow I just found it really hard to believe that the claw wasn't going to turn up *somewhere*."

"But what led you to Buster?" asked Maggie.

"Like I said, it was the licorice gum that first tipped me off," said Fenton. "And once I remembered Buster's black bubble, I got to thinking about everything else that happened that day in the hall after school—especially about all that stuff Buster said to me. I mean, it was pretty confusing at the time, but I definitely got the feeling that Buster thought I was trying to get to him in some way."

"But how could you have been trying to get to him?" asked Maggie. "You didn't know anything yet."

"Well, remember earlier that day in science when Mrs. Rigby asked me about the iguanodon skeleton?" asked Fenton.

"Sure," said Maggie. "You told that cool story about the two brothers and the iguanodon tail."

"I think Buster was convinced that I was talking about stolen fossils like that because I wanted to let him know I was onto him."

"So that's why he threatened you in the hall," said Maggie.

"Right," said Fenton. "Then I began to think back to that day at the dig site, and I realized that Buster could easily have taken the claw when he was in the trailer. All he needed was somewhere to put it."

"The yellow knapsack!" said Willy.

"Exactly," said Fenton. "The yellow knapsack was Matt's, not Buster's. Matt just happened to bring it to the dig site."

"Which is why Buster wasn't carrying it when we arrived," said Maggie, nodding.

"But then later, when Buster needed someplace to put the claw he had stolen, he must have made Matt give him his knapsack," explained Fenton.

"That's why Buster was guarding it so carefully on the bus," said Maggie. "Wow, you sure did some good sleuthing on this, Fen."

Fenton looked at her.

"What did you just call me?" he asked.

"What I always call you," she said, biting into another rib. "Fen. Why, don't you like having a nickname?"

Fenton grinned. He liked it just fine.